Mistaken Identity

by

Jeanne Riedel

Strategic Book Publishing and Rights Co.

This is a work of fiction. Names, characters, places, and incidents either are a product of the author's imagination or are used fictitiously, and any resemblance to actual persons, living or dead, business establishments, events, or locales is entirely coincidental.

Book Design/Layout by Kalpart. Visit www.kalpart.com

Strategic Book Publishing and Rights Co.
12620 FM 1960, Suite A4-507
Houston TX 77065
www.sbpra.com

ISBN: 978-1-60976-906-2

Dedication

This novel is dedicated to Cindy, my friend and partner in crime.

We have been friends forever and she has been my sounding board whenever I came up with an idea for my writing. Also, for all her support through the years.

To my family, I appreciate all your support as I worked on getting my novel published.

I would also like to thank Carla, Sondra, and Jeanie for taking the time to read my novel and help me with the editing.

Chapter One

Emily turned the corner and pulled up next to the curb. She sat gazing at the huge three-story Victorian house down the block. Liz had always wanted to own a Victorian home, and she finally made her dream come true. It had a wraparound porch with a swing hanging from the ceiling of the porch. It looked like the turret had windows on all sides. Grabbing her camera from the seat next to her, Emily got out and walked to the front of the car.

After taking a couple of shots of the entire house, Emily put on her telephoto lens to take some close up shots. She wanted to get more detail of the gingerbread trim above the porch and around the gabled windows. Liz had given her instructions on photography when they were together two years ago, and she was eager for her to see how she had progressed with picture taking. Even though Emily used a digital camera, Liz was going to teach her how to develop pictures manually. Liz had told her that the first thing she did after moving into the house was to make the spare room next to her office into a darkroom.

The lot next to the house also belonged to Liz. It had an arbor that led from the backyard to a nice area with red maple trees and a few fruit trees. There were a couple of adirondack chairs under a huge maple tree with a small table between them. It looked like a good place to sit and enjoy a summer evening.

Raising her camera, she took a few more pictures of the area. The woods behind the lot added to the ambience of the scene. The house seemed to be out in the country instead of in town. There were only a couple of houses across the street and just wide-open spaces behind her. Emily always liked the feel of a small town even though she had lived in Kansas City for a while.

Returning to her vehicle Emily proceeded up the street. She stopped her car by a big maple tree and got out so that she could take a few pictures of the front of the house and the very inviting wraparound porch with the swing. She walked across the street to get a better shot.

Enough pictures for now, she just wanted to see Liz and give her a great big hug. It had been much too long since they had seen each other. They talked on the phone every week, but that wasn't the same as talking in person. After putting her camera in the trunk of her car, Emily grabbed her purse and hurried up the steps to the front door.

Ringing the doorbell, Emily eagerly waited for Liz to answer. As she looked around to the front windows, she was surprised that the curtains were not open. Glancing at her watch, she saw that it was 9:30. Liz was always an early riser, and the first thing she would do was open her curtains and let the light in.

Emily rang the bell a second time. Getting impatient, she went down the steps and looked up at the second and third stories of the house. Perhaps if she were up on the third floor, it would take her a while to get down here to answer the door. Not getting an answer again, Emily went to the back yard to see if Liz was working there. The garage was open with Liz's car inside, but there was no sign of her.

"Okay Liz, stop playing games. You knew I would be here this morning, so just open the door." Pulling open the screen door, Emily turned the knob on the inside door. It opened easily.

Sticking her head inside, Emily called out, "Liz, it's Emily. Where are you?"

Stepping all the way inside, Emily closed the door quietly behind her and waited a few seconds for Liz to respond to her call. It took her eyes a minute to adjust to the dark. The coolness of the entry made her shiver.

Placing her purse on the table next to the door, Emily slowly entered the room. Liz's purse was hanging on the banister, so she must be around somewhere.

"Liz, this isn't funny. Come on out!" Emily called as she walked toward the stairs.

Something was wrong Emily thought as another shiver ran down her spine. Everything was still closed up which wasn't like Liz at all. She enjoyed the morning light and the fresh air. The quiet of the house sent an eerie feeling to the pit of her stomach. Emily checked the room off the entry. A door was open at the far end of the room.

"Liz, are you in there?" Emily called again as she went to check the open door.

Turning on the light, she discovered that it was Liz's darkroom. There were trays with some kind of solution in them and several pictures hanging to dry. After going back out to the entry, Emily walked down the hall toward the back of the house. She came to the kitchen, which was as neat as a pin. Things just didn't feel right.

Back at the bottom of the stairs, she decided to check out the second and third floors. Maybe Liz was in one of the backrooms and didn't hear her call. The creak of the first step unnerved her. It shattered the silence and seemed to reverberate throughout the house. Emily's heart began to pound. Something was terribly wrong.

Pausing on the landing, she called out again, "Liz, if this is your idea of a joke, it's not funny." She waited, hoping that Liz would appear at the top of the stairs laughing. There was absolutely no sound coming from the floor above.

Taking a deep breath, Emily continued up to the second floor. At the top she peered down the hallway where there were four rooms. Walking down the hall, she looked into the rooms one at a time. Most of the rooms had boxes and other items stored in them. Upon reaching the room at the end of the hall, Emily slowly opened the door. Liz was lying on the bed.

"Didn't you hear me calling you?" Emily said as she entered the room. Not getting a response, she rushed over to the bed.

"Liz, wake up," Emily said, shaking her.

She could feel panic begin to swell up inside her. Taking a deep breath she worked to calm herself down. The first thing was to check for a pulse. Not finding any, Emily picked up the phone by the bed to call 911.

"Please send an ambulance as quickly as possible! My friend won't wake up. The address is 1704 Maple Street. No, I don't know what's wrong. I just got here and found her unconscious. I wasn't able to find a pulse. Please hurry."

Placing the phone back on the nightstand, Emily knocked something off. When she picked it up, she saw that it was a prescription bottle. "Sleeping pills," she said reading the label. "Why in the world would Liz have a prescription for sleeping pills? She hates them."

Things just didn't make any sense at all. Emily paced around the room waiting for the EMS to arrive. "Where are they?" She thought glancing at her watch. It had only been a couple of minutes since she called, but it seemed like it had been hours. Hearing sirens, Emily hurried out of the room and down the stairs.

"Please hurry!" Emily called as the first EMT came up on the porch. "She is on the second floor. The last room on the right."

Emily started to follow the men up the stairs when she felt a light touch on her arm.

"May I ask you a few questions?"

"Who are you?" Emily asked, startled to see someone else had come into the house.

"I'm Detective Daniels, and I need to ask you a few questions about what happened here."

"I'm sorry, Detective, but I really need to be with my friend and find out how she's doing." Emily turned to head up the stairs, but was stopped by the officer who had come in behind Detective Daniels.

"Look, Miss, I know you're worried about your friend, but I do need to ask you some questions. Officer Jones will go upstairs to see how she is doing. Why don't we just go over here and sit down." Detective Daniels took Emily by the arm and led her to the couch.

"What is your name?" Detective Daniels asked taking a notepad and pen out of his pocket.

"My name is Emily Jansen." Emily continued to look toward the stairs. What was going on up there?

"What is the name of the person upstairs?"

"Her name is Liz Marshall."

"And how do you know Miss Marshall?

"Liz and I have been friends since grade school. I came here to spend the summer with her." She sure wished she knew what was taking them so long.

The EMTs had no problem finding Liz's room. They rushed to the bed and tried to find a pulse. "I'm not finding a pulse. Let's try CPR." They took her off the bed and placed her on the floor. After trying for several minutes to revive her and not getting a pulse, they gave up. Placing her body on the stretcher, they covered her with a sheet.

The officer looked around the room for clues as to what had happened. Noticing the empty bottle on the nightstand, he took out a small bag and placed the bottle inside.

"This looks like the cause of death," he remarked holding up the bag with the empty bottle of sleeping pills. "My initial prediction would be suicide. It doesn't look like anything is amiss," he concluded, and checked the bathroom, where everything was neat and tidy.

"Detective Daniels, could I see you for a moment?" the officer called from the top of the stairs down to where the detective was talking to Emily.

"Excuse me, Miss, I'll be right back." Detective Daniels went upstairs to talk to the other officer. "What have you got?"

Holding up the plastic bag with the empty pill bottle, he said, "Looks like suicide. I didn't find a note, but this very much indicates that possibility."

"You're wrong! Liz would never kill herself!" Emily exclaimed vehemently.

Startled, both men turned to see Emily standing a few feet from them. "Liz hated pills; she would never take sleeping pills."

"Now, Miss Jansen, we haven't made any definite conclusions. That will be up to the coroner to decide. Why don't we go back downstairs and let them finish doing their job."

Back in the living room Emily sat on the couch placing her head in her hands. She couldn't believe what was happening. Not even an hour ago she had been so excited to see Liz and spend the summer with her, and now everything was turned upside down.

"Miss Jansen, I just have a couple more questions. I know this is very difficult for you, but I do have to ask them."

"Whatever, let's just get this over with." Emily ran her fingers through her hair and leaned back on the couch.

"How did you get into the house?"

The front door opening and closing stopped Emily from answering the question. Detective Daniels got up to see who had come in. Emily followed him to the entryway.

"Glad you're here Dr. Berry. The body is in the bedroom

upstairs at the end of the hallway," Detective Daniels said quietly hoping Emily would not hear.

"The body does have a name and that is Liz," Emily stated vehemently.

Dr. Berry was surprised by the outburst. "Excuse me Miss, I'll just go upstairs." He hurried up the stairs and out of sight.

"Another one of your detectives?" Emily asked. " I wish you would quit making Liz seem like just another thing. She is a person not an object." Emily struggled to hold in the tears. She didn't want to breakdown in front of Detective Daniels.

"I'm sorry, Miss Jansen, Dr. Berry is the coroner. Now can we get back to the question?" Daniels said, fumbling with his notebook.

"Oh, okay." Shaking her head Emily continued, "I don't seem to remember the question."

"How did you get into the house."

"The door was unlocked."

"Is your friend in the habit of leaving her door unlocked?"

"No, she isn't. Even though this is a small town, she told me she would keep her doors locked when she wasn't downstairs. 'Now a days you can't be too careful' she would always say. I was surprised it was unlocked since the curtains were closed."

"Is there any one you want us to contact?"

"There's no one to call. Liz didn't have any family. I need some air." Emily got up and walked outside to the porch. Resting her hands on the railing, she fought to keep the tears inside. With several deep breaths, she tried to calm her nerves.

She noticed two officers putting up yellow crime scene tape. Why would they do that if she committed suicide?

"It's just routine," Detective Daniels said noticing Emily's puzzled look. "We do that even if a suicide is suspected until the autopsy can be performed to determine for sure the cause of death."

Emily leaned against the post and watched as they brought Liz's body out and placed her in the ambulance. It was very unnerving to watch it drive away without the siren blaring.

"Miss Jansen, it's time to go."

The sound of his voice startled her, "I'm sorry, what did you say?"

"They're all finished here, and we need to lock up. Do you have someplace to go?"

"I don't know. I guess I'll have to find a hotel. I had been planning on staying with Liz. But that's out of the question now."

"There's a nice little bed and breakfast just a few blocks from here. If you want to follow me in your car, I'll show you where it is."

"Thank you, I appreciate your help. I just need to get my purse from inside the house."

Emily glanced around the entryway and up the stairs. A shiver ran down her spine. Quickly she turned to get back out into the sunshine. She suddenly felt very cold.

Detective Daniels walked with Emily to her car. "If you wait just a moment, I'll be right back, and then I'll show you to the bed and breakfast.

Emily just nodded as she got into her car. Staring at the house, she wondered what really happened. Liz did not commit suicide; she knew that for a fact. She would just have to prove it to the police. It wasn't long before Detective Daniels came back, and she followed him to the bed and breakfast.

They stopped in front of a quaint two-story rock house. The stone looked to be limestone. It looked like it had been built around the turn of the century. The front door had an old-fashioned screen door painted green, and the inside door contained a beautiful large frosted oval glass. The front porch ran the entire length of the house. A swing, along with a couple of white wooden rocking chairs, adorned the porch inviting guests to enjoy a beautiful summer evening.

Emily opened the trunk of her car to get out a couple of suitcases. Detective Daniels was there to help before she could reach for them herself.

"Thank you."

"I'll take them inside for you."

"You don't have to do that," Emily replied, quickly taking her bags. "I can manage from here."

"You'll have to make a statement for our records, but you can do that either later today or tomorrow morning. Whichever is convenient for you?" Detective Daniels felt sorry for this young woman. This definitely was no way to begin a visit to a friend.

"How soon will you have the autopsy report?"

"If everything is routine, and they don't find anything unusual, then we could have the results in a day or two. The body will be released to you as soon as they are done with the autopsy."

Emily didn't like referring to Liz as "THE BODY." She couldn't believe that she would be planning Liz's funeral instead of helping her fix up her house. What a strange twist of fate.

"Thank you, Detective Daniels, for all your help. I'll come down to the police station later today and give you my statement."

Detective Daniels nodded and then turned to get into his car.

Emily made her way up the sidewalk and then proceeded up the steps of the Willow Tree Bed and Breakfast. Hopefully they had a vacancy. Emily walked to the far end of what appeared to be the parlor to the check in desk. No one was around, so she rang the bell.

A woman appeared wiping her hands on her bright floral apron. She must have been working in the kitchen. She had her hair up in a bun on the top of her head, and she smelled of cinnamon.

"Hi, I'm Margaret Bennett, but everyone calls me Maggie. You must be Emily." Maggie said reaching out her hand.

"How did you know?" Emily asked in total surprise automatically shaking her hand.

"Adam, Detective Daniels, called and said he was bringing you by. He told me briefly what happened. I'm very sorry."

"Thank you," Emily remarked quietly.

"I do have two rooms available. One room has a private bath and the other you would share a bath with another room."

"The room with the private bath, please." Emily didn't want to share a bathroom. She wanted her privacy.

"How long will you be staying?"

How long would she be staying? Emily had no idea. "I guess three nights for right now. If, I decide to stay longer, will the room be available?"

"That will be no problem. We can talk more about it in a couple of days. Now, just fill out this card, and I'll show you to your room."

Emily filled out the card and followed Maggie up the stairs. Maggie was giving her a brief history of the house. She tried to listen, but wasn't having much luck.

"Here we are. You'll be staying in the Rose Room. Here's the key. I'll be downstairs if you need anything."

Emily stood staring at the bed. The events of the last few hours were slowly sinking in now that she was alone. The tears she had kept inside streamed down her cheeks. Setting her suitcases on the floor, Emily dropped onto the bed and let the tears flow.

Emily stared up at the ceiling. The tears were gone, but the ache of her loss was still very fresh. Sitting up, her head began to pound. It felt as though there were a big bass drum pounding inside. Reaching for her purse, Emily dumped the contents onto the bed. She knew she had some aspirin somewhere. Rifling through the items, Emily found the small case that held her pills. Picking it up she went into the bathroom for a glass of water. She washed the pills down with the water. Carrying the glass, she went back into the bedroom and sat on the bed, placing the glass on the nightstand.

A vision of Liz's bedroom came to her mind as she stared at the glass. There was no glass on the nightstand. How could anyone take a bottle of pills and not drink a glass of water. Besides Liz hated sleeping pills. There was just no way that she would take sleeping pills. Especially not after what happened to her father.

Throwing everything back into her purse, Emily knew she had to talk to Detective Daniels right away. There was no way that Liz killed herself. She would never take a bottle of sleeping pills. Putting her purse on her shoulder, she went out into the hallway and hurried down the steps.

If she remembered correctly, the police station was on Main Street. Emily pulled away from the curb and turned at the next corner. She drove another two blocks and came to Main. She wasn't sure which direction to turn, but decided to go left. If she didn't find it, she would just turn around and go the other direction. After driving about a block, Emily stopped in front of the police station.

Taking a deep breath, Emily fought to control the tears that were once again threatening to overflow. She was determined not to let Detective Daniels see her cry. Taking a tissue from her purse, she dabbed her eyes and blew her nose. After taking one more deep breath she opened the car door and got out.

"May I speak to Detective Daniels?" Emily asked the officer behind the counter as confidently as she could.

The station was the typical small town station. There were just three desks behind the counter. Two doors lead to other rooms, and one seemed to lead back to the jail area of the station.

The officer she had spoken to had gone into one of the

rooms and then emerged signaling her. She walked over to the office and thanked the officer before entering the room. Detective Daniels was seated behind his rather messy desk, but he rose as Emily entered the room.

"Please have a seat, Miss Jansen. I didn't expect you so soon."

"Before I give my statement, I would like to give you a little information about Liz that should help you realize that she wouldn't kill herself, especially by taking a bottle of sleeping pills."

"What kind of information do you have that would change my conclusion in this matter?" Detective Daniels crossed his arms in front of him and leaned back in his chair.

Emily sensed right away that he wouldn't believe anything she said, but she was going to try. She had to change his mind.

"In your report, Detective, did it mention the items that were on Liz's nightstand?"

Daniels picked up a report and began reading through it. "It says here that the items on the nightstand were one lamp, an alarm clock, a box of tissues, and an empty prescription bottle for sleeping pills."

"It doesn't say anything about a glass of water?"

"No." Detective Daniels looked at her quizzically. "What's the importance of a glass of water?"

"If you were going to take a bottle of pills, wouldn't you want to have a glass of water? I know I would."

"Yeh, I suppose I would. So?"

"There was no glass of water on the nightstand."

"Maybe she took them in the bathroom and left the glass in there."

"Why would someone take a whole bottle of pills in the bathroom and then carry the empty bottle back to the bed and put it on the nightstand?"

"People who kill themselves don't think rationally, Miss Jansen," Detective Daniels remarked, sitting up and leaning on the desk.

"That may be true, but there is another reason I know that Liz did not take those pills."

"And what reason would that be?" Detective Daniels was getting a little tired of all this supposition even though he felt sorry for Emily.

"The reason, Detective Daniels, has to do with Liz's childhood. When she was about ten years old, her father killed himself by taking a bottle of sleeping pills. Liz was the one who found him. She was the one who called the ambulance. Her mother was working late that night. That memory stuck with her, and since then she has been deathly afraid of taking sleeping pills. Even when she was going through a period when she wasn't sleeping and her doctor wanted to prescribe sleeping pills, she refused to take them."

"That's all very well, Miss Jansen, but that may be the exact reason she took sleeping pills to end her life. She knew it worked for her father, so she was going to be like him."

Shaking her head Emily reiterated, "No, no, she would not kill herself by taking sleeping pills. She would not kill herself period. Liz was looking forward to this summer and having me here to help her fix up the house."

"How long has it been since you have seen Liz?"

"It has been two years since we have seen each other, but we talked every week. I just talked to her last night and she was very excited about my being here. She just bought that old Victorian house about a month ago and was planning on turning it into a bed and breakfast. Does that sound like someone who wanted to commit suicide?" Emily used all her willpower to hold her tears in check. There was no way she was going to let him see her cry.

"Look, Miss Jansen, if it will make you feel better, I'll double check what the officers on the scene found and make sure that nothing was missed. That's the best I can do."

"Thank you," Emily replied quietly. "I guess I had better give you my statement."

"That can wait until tomorrow. Right now why don't you go back to the bed and breakfast and just relax?"

Emily glanced at her watch. It was almost four o'clock. She hadn't eaten anything since last night and was beginning to get hungry. "I guess that would be a good idea. I'll come by in the morning and give you my statement."

"That will be just fine. I'll check things out to see if there is anything the officers missed."

"Thank you."

The summer sun was bright and warm, but despite its warmth Emily felt a chill as she stood on the sidewalk outside the police station. The growling of her stomach brought her back to reality. Seeing a sign for a café in the next block, she decided to get a bite to eat. Leaving her car where it was, she just walked the short distance to the café.

Stepping inside, she stood waiting for her eyes to adjust. There was a bar on the far right with big, round, red seats that swiveled. A row of booths was situated on the wall opposite the door. There were about eight to ten tables with red and white-checkered tablecloths. The dining area looked like it could hold about 25-30 people. The walls were covered with local memorabilia.

Emily picked a booth that was farthest from the bar. The room was almost empty since it was early for the dinner crowd. She was glad of the solitude. The bustle of a crowd was not what she was interested in.

The waitress brought her a menu and a glass of water. "Would you care for anything to drink?"

"Tea, no lemon, please."

Emily looked over the menu. Nothing sounded good, but she knew she had to eat something. The standard cheeseburger and salad would do.

"What can I get for you?" the waitress asked taking a notepad and pencil from her apron pocket.

Emily forced a smile and replied, "I'll just have a cheeseburger and salad with thousand island dressing on the side."

"I'll be right back with your drink."

The waitress brought her drink along with a straw. Emily judged her to be in her teens. It was probably a summer job for her. From where she was sitting, she could look back into the kitchen area. There seemed to be one cook and just three others including her waitress getting ready for the dinner crowd.

The picture on the wall above her booth showed beautifully dressed men and women dancing in a large ballroom. Even though it was a black and white photo, you could see the richness of the dresses that were worn.

As Emily began eating, a few people began to trickle into the café. Everyone seemed to know each other, which was typical in a small town. A couple of women sat at the booth next to hers and began whispering.

"Did you hear about Liz Marshall? Someone found her body this morning in her house!"

"I know. They say she committed suicide. Did you know her?"

"Not very well."

"Me neither. You wonder what makes someone do something like that."

Emily had just taken a couple of bites of her food when she realized that they were talking about Liz. Her stomach turned into knots, and her appetite disappeared. How in the world would people know about what had happened to Liz? Shaking her head, she realized this was a small town, and bad news traveled fast.

Emily quickly paid her bill and exited the café. The weather was warm with a gentle breeze rustling through the trees. Not wanting to be cooped up in her room, Emily decided to go for a walk. As she walked along, the sound of children faintly filled the air.

Looking around, Emily found herself standing in a park. The peacefulness that filled the air flowed through her. Finding a bench among a group of trees, Emily sat down to let the peace and solitude envelope her. Closing her eyes, she let the breeze blow gently across her face. But, with the closing of her eyes, the picture of Liz in her bedroom came creeping in. Shaking her head, she tried to get rid of that picture. As soon as she had the funeral for Liz she would head back home. She didn't want to stay here any longer than she had too.

Back at her car Emily decided to return to the Willow Tree. The streets were filled with more activity. People were out walking, and the kids were enjoying their summer vacation. Everyone looked so happy.

Parking her car in front of the Willow Tree, Emily just sat staring out the window after turning off the engine. She knew she would eventually get through this, but it sure wouldn't be easy.

Walking up the front steps, Emily spotted the swing at the end of the porch. It looked very inviting, and since no one was around, she made herself comfortable. The rocking of the swing was very relaxing. Closing her eyes, she thought of all the fun things she and Liz had done. They did get into mischief once in awhile.

"You must be having some very pleasant thoughts."

The male voice surprised her. Opening her eyes, she saw a gentleman leaning against the railing of the porch with his arms crossed in front of him. He looked to be in his mid thirties with wavy brown hair and a boyish grin.

"I'm sorry, I didn't mean to startle you. It's just that whatever or whomever you were thinking about seemed to make you happy."

"It did," Emily said quietly, trying to keep her voice from shaking hiding the tears in her eyes.

"I'm sorry, I didn't mean to upset you," the gentleman said, sitting on the swing next to her.

"You didn't do anything, really. I have to go now." Emily got up from the swing and went inside to her room leaving the gentleman staring after her.

Back in her room, Emily kicked off her shoes and noticed a vase filled with yellow roses sitting on the nightstand. Roses for the rose room she thought walking into the bathroom.

Needing to unwind, Emily filled the big claw foot tub. Pouring vanilla scented bubble bath into the running water, she breathed in the relaxing fragrance. Placing a washcloth on the rim, Emily carefully stepped into the hot water and bubbles. Leaning back and resting her head on the washcloth, she closed her eyes and tried to forget the events of the day. The soothing scent, and the hot water did begin to make her feel relaxed. She just sat in the tub not wanting to move. The water started to get cold, and reluctantly Emily got out of the tub.

After wrapping herself up in her bathrobe, Emily sat on the window seat and watched as the sky turned shades of purple and pink from the setting sun. The colors were so vibrant. Too bad her camera was in the trunk of her car. As the colors faded, the first stars of the evening began to appear. The night looked so peaceful. Too bad she didn't feel that way inside. With nothing to do, she crawled into bed hoping sleep would overtake her quickly.

Even though she was exhausted, Emily was unable to fall asleep. Turning on the lamp on the nightstand, she wondered if she could make herself a cup of tea. It was only ten thirty; maybe Maggie was still up so she could ask her.

The house was quiet as Emily stepped into the hall. Her slippered feet let her walk quietly down the stairs to the first floor. A light shone in the dining room. Maggie was seated at the table sipping on what appeared to be a cup of coffee and paging through a magazine.

"Hi, Maggie, mind if I join you?" Emily asked as she walked into the room.

"Sure, would you like a cup of coffee?"

"Actually, I was hoping to have a cup of chamomile tea"

"No problem. Why don't you follow me into the kitchen so we can visit while the water is heating."

Emily took a seat at the island in the middle of the room. It was a fairly large room with a small breakfast nook and a bay window. The ceiling above the island had a rack with pots and pans hanging on it. The stove was a big gas stove with six burners and a huge oven. Cabinets above the counter were painted a dark green with glass front doors. Everything looked very organized.

Taking a deep breath, Emily could still smell the lingering scent of freshly baked cinnamon rolls. Her stomach growled a little letting her know that she hadn't eaten much that day.

Maggie sat down opposite Emily. Reaching across the counter, she patted her on the hand. "I'm very sorry about your friend."

"I don't believe that she committed suicide. Liz wouldn't do something like that. She was looking forward to my spending the summer with her and helping her fix up her house. I'm really the only family she had, so she was happy I was coming."

"Could she have been distraught over something that you didn't know about?"

"No, we always told each other everything. She hated sleeping pills. There is no way she would have done something like that."

The teakettle began to whistle. Maggie got up and poured hot water over the tea bag in the cup. She placed the cup along with a cinnamon roll in front of Emily.

"Thank you. I guess I am a little hungry. I haven't had much to eat today." Emily took a bite of the roll that just melted in her mouth. "It is delicious."

"Thank you."

Taking a sip of her tea Emily let the warm liquid slide down her throat. "This has hit the spot."

"So, Emily, you really don't think Liz killed herself."

"No, I don't." Emily said shaking her head.

"You know what that means if she didn't commit suicide, don't you?"

"I don't understand."

If she didn't kill herself, and the autopsy shows that she died from an overdose of sleeping pills, that would mean that someone had killed her."

"Good evening, ladies. May I join you?"

It was the gentleman from the porch. How much of their conversation had he over heard? Emily concentrated on eating her roll avoiding looking at him.

"Would you like a cup of coffee or tea, Mr. Baker?" Maggie asked him trying to cover Emily's uneasiness.

A cup of tea would be fine since it looks like you already have water heated." He sat on the stool next to Emily. "I'm sorry if I interrupted your conversation."

"You didn't interrupt. I was just about to take my tea and roll up to my room to finish. Good night, Maggie. Good night, Mr. Baker." Emily fled the room without looking back.

"Good night, Emily." Maggie watched her walk out through the kitchen door and disappear around the corner. "Poor thing." She shook her head while pouring Mr. Baker's cup of tea.

"Why poor thing?"

"She came to Hampton today to spend the summer with her friend."

"That sounds like it would be something exciting. Not something bad."

"When she got to her friend's house, she found her friend

dead. She apparently committed suicide only Emily doesn't think her friend would kill herself."

"That is tough."

"Emily has to handle everything herself because Liz has no family to speak of."

In the safety of her room Emily sipped on her tea and finished the roll Maggie had given her. Maggie's words echoed in her head. "If she didn't commit suicide, then she must have been murdered." That thought had never crossed her mind, but Liz didn't kill herself so she must have been murdered. This was too much for her to take in, all in one day.

The scent of roses slowly filled Emily's nostrils. It was such a sweet soothing smell. She noticed the yellow roses on her nightstand had a card with them that she hadn't seen earlier. Opening the card, Emily saw that it was from Maggie. It simply said, "I'm sorry for your loss. Maggie"

Tears welled up in her eyes. That was very sweet of someone she had just met. Pulling her legs up close to her chest, she rested her head on her knees to try and comfort herself. She had never felt so alone as she did at that moment.

The morning sun streaming in the window woke Emily. Picking up the clock on the nightstand, she saw it was almost seven. Falling back on the pillow, she covered her eyes with her arm. She wished she could wave a magic wand and put everything back the way it was supposed to be. That wasn't going to happen. She would have to deal with things no matter how she felt. May as well get going.

Even though she had taken a bubble bath last night, she thought a hot shower would help her get ready to face what lay ahead. Water flowing over her body helped her feel human. By the time Emily had finished getting ready, she was prepared to face Detective Daniels and give him her statement.

Emily noticed a faint scent of bacon and eggs as she grabbed her purse to go downstairs. Her stomach growled, and she remembered that she hadn't eaten much the day before.

"Good morning. Emily," Maggie said as she walked into the dining room. "Would you like some breakfast?"

"As a matter of fact, I would. I didn't eat much yesterday and I'm starved."

"Good. Sit down at the table, and I'll bring you a plate."

There was hot water for tea setting on the sideboard. Emily helped herself and then sat at the table. Maggie brought her a plate full of food and placed it in front of her.

"I don't know if I can eat all this," Emily exclaimed looking at the plate of food. There were scrambled eggs, bacon and sausage, hash browns, and two pieces of toast.

"You just eat. And don't worry about how much is on your plate. If you didn't eat much yesterday, then you need all this nourishment," Maggie said patting Emily on the arm. "Would you like some orange juice with that also?"

"Yes, thank you very much."

"It's nice to see a woman who isn't afraid to eat," Jack Baker said as he sat down at the table opposite of Emily.

"Good morning," Emily said trying to be pleasant.

"I'm sorry about your friend. If there's anything I can do to help, please let me know."

"Thank you, Mr. Baker."

"Please call me Jack, and I hope I can call you Emily," Jack replied flashing his boyish grin.

Emily couldn't help but smile. "Okay, Jack, and, yes, you may call me Emily."

"I thought I heard your voice, Mr. Baker. I fixed a plate for you. I know how you like your breakfast." Maggie set a plate in front of him.

Emily thought her plate was full, but his had twice as much on it.

"Now, Maggie, I always tell you to call me Jack. You like to tease me and call me Mr. Baker, don't you?" Jack remarked squeezing Maggie's hand.

Emily watched as Maggie blushed at Jack's teasing and mild flirtation. After Maggie went back into the kitchen, Emily asked, "Are you a frequent visitor to the Willow Tree?"

"Yes, I am. How did you know?"

"The way you and Maggie tease each other made me figure that you have known each other for a while."

"You're right. I'm usually here about once every two months or so on business."

Emily finished her breakfast and thanked Maggie for the delicious meal. She wanted to get to the police station, so she could give her statement to Detective Daniels and talk to him about Liz.

When she reached the police station, there was a man talking with Detective Daniels. She sat in a chair by the door and decided to wait until they were finished. The Detective was listening intently to the man and took a piece of paper from him. He nodded his head, and the man turned to leave. Emily didn't recognize him as he went out the door. Detective Daniels waved her over to his office.

"Good morning, Miss Jansen. Please have a seat."

"Thank you. I'm ready to give you my statement."

Emily recreated what happened the day before when she arrived at Liz's to spend the summer. As she told her story, the detective took notes. There really wasn't a whole lot to tell, and it didn't take very long for her to finish. "As I said yesterday, Detective, Liz could not have killed herself because she hated sleeping pills. There would be no way that she would take one, let alone a whole bottle."

"I'm afraid, Miss Jansen, that we have positive proof that your friend committed suicide," Detective Daniels said quietly.

"What kind of proof?" Emily could not believe what she was hearing.

"First, the preliminary report from the coroner is death by an overdose of sleeping pills. He will complete his findings by the end of the day, and we should have his complete report then."

"You said 'first', is there something else?"

"The gentleman that was just in here when you arrived was Lee Masters. He received this in the mail this morning." Detective Daniels handed her a note.

"What's this?"

"It is a note Liz wrote to Lee Masters before she killed herself."

Emily read the note. This could not be true. She knew Liz, and there was no way she could have done this.

Lee,

I wanted to tell you that Julia didn't run away, I killed her. I am sorry. I have lived with this guilt for too long and can no longer go on. I hope someday you will find it in your heart to forgive me.

Liz

"That note gives us the reason she did it. With the preliminary report from the coroner, the only conclusion I can come to is that she committed suicide.

"But how do you know for sure that the note is from Liz? It most likely was done on a computer. Anyone could have done it." Emily would not believe that Liz had killed another person. The situation was just getting stranger by the minute.

"Is this her signature?"

"It looks like her writing, but that doesn't mean she wrote it. She might have been forced to write it. Is the address written or typed?"

"Both addresses were typed."

"Doesn't that prove that someone else could have sent that letter?"

"I'm sorry, Miss Jansen, my report is going to say suicide as the cause of death."

"I will never believe that Liz killed herself. When she was ten years old, she found her father dead from an overdose of sleeping pills. She hated sleeping pills and would never take them."

"The prescription was in her name."

Shaking her head, "She did not kill herself and I intend on proving it."

"I'm very sorry, Miss Jansen."

Emily bit her bottom lip to keep from crying. "When will Liz's body be released so that I can plan her funeral?"

"Her body should be released later today since the coroner should have his report done by the end of the day."

"I'll call you later with the name of the funeral home." Detective Daniels just nodded. "Thank you for all your help Detective, even though you're wrong about Liz." Emily left the police station in a daze. She couldn't believe all this was happening.

Chapter Two

Emily watched the policeman as he removed the yellow crime scene tape from around Liz's property. She was surprised when a white pickup pulled into the driveway. The man that got out was the same one who had been in the police station talking to Detective Daniels just a few hours earlier. So this was Lee Masters. She did remember seeing him when she visited Liz two years ago. What was he doing here? Even with her window down, she was parked too far away to hear their conversation.

Emily saw Lee point to the house, and the officer shakes his head no. What in the world did he want? It wasn't long before he got back into his pickup and drove away. The officer finished taking down the tape and then got into his patrol car and left.

After a couple of minutes, Emily got out of her car. She looked around to make sure no one was watching and walked quickly to the chairs that were under the maple tree. From there she again looked around and then hurried through the arbor to the back yard. No one would see her back there especially with the woods behind the yard.

Liz had told her about a key hidden behind a loose piece of siding right by the back porch. It took her a few tries to find the loose piece and move it to get to the key. Once she found it she made sure no one was looking, unlocked the back door and let herself into the house. If she couldn't find Liz's keys, she would keep this one and use it to get in the house. Emily put the key in a zippered section of her purse so that she wouldn't lose it.

She found herself standing in a little entryway or what would now be called a mudroom. There were hooks on the wall to hang coats and scarves. There was a rubber mat on the floor under the hooks where one could put wet shoes. Going through the door she entered the kitchen. There were two doors to the left of her and one to the right. One was the laundry room. Everything was very neat except for the lid of the washing machine. It was not closed completely. Opening the lid Emily saw that there were several towels in the machine, and the corner of one was not all the way down in the drum of the machine. The towels were damp, so they must have been put in the machine while wet, which must have been yesterday.

Emily left the towels as they were and proceeded to check out the other door. That one led to the basement. The basement could wait. She was more interested in finding evidence that Liz was murdered. Everything was as neat as a pin. Nothing was out of place. There was no cup or spoon in the sink or the dishwasher. No sign that she had made herself a cup of tea.

Before leaving the kitchen, Emily checked out the last door. This was the broom closet. Everything looked fine.

Liz's routine was the same every day. She would come downstairs, unlock her door to check for the paper, open the curtains, and then make herself a cup of tea. Her routine must have been interrupted, but by whom.

Then again, they say people do strange things before they kill themselves. Maybe she washed everything up and put it away before going back upstairs to take the sleeping pills. Emily shook her head. Liz did not kill herself. There had to be another explanation and she was determined to find it.

At the bottom of the stairs Emily hesitated before going up. The only way to prove that Liz was murdered was for her to go back upstairs to Liz's room and search for clues. The silence in the house was deafening, so the creaking of the floor as she stepped onto the landing made her jump. The sound echoed throughout the house causing her heart to race. She knew she was alone, but she couldn't help looking over her shoulder to make sure.

All the doors were closed just like yesterday when she first arrived. Her steps slowed the closer she got to Liz's bedroom. She really didn't want to go back in there, but she knew she had to look for clues.

The coldness of the doorknob as she turned it sent a shiver down her spine. The bedroom was cool despite the warmth outside. She left the door wide open, so she could easily escape if she had to. There is nothing to be afraid of she told herself as she hung her purse on the doorknob. The bed loomed in front of her. She shivered again thinking of Liz lying there.

Looking around, everything was almost too neat. Liz was a meticulous housekeeper, but there wasn't anything out of place. There wasn't a tissue on the nightstand or in the wastebasket next to the bed. In the adjoining bathroom, there were no bath towels, hand towels, or washcloths out. Would Liz have taken all the towels downstairs and then come back up to take the pills?

Things didn't make any sense. Why didn't she get dressed? Why didn't she dry her hair? Did she take the bottle of pills, drink some water and then go into the bathroom and set the glass back on the sink. Picking up the glass, she noticed that there were no water spots. The glass drying by itself would show some water spots, but there were none.

Opening the cupboard under the sink, Emily found the wastebasket. There again, empty. There were no tissues, cotton balls, nothing. The only sign of anything was the prescription bottle left on the nightstand for someone to find so it could be called a suicide. The police had taken it for evidence, so it was no longer there.

The bedspread was slightly mussed where Liz had been lying. Touching the bedspread Emily said, "Oh, Liz, what happened in here yesterday?" She shivered as goose bumps ran up her arms. Taking her purse from the doorknob, she closed the door to go back downstairs.

Walking down the hall, she checked out the other rooms. All had boxes that had not yet been opened. One room also had a mattress and box springs in it along with several boxes. The bedroom closest to the stairs had French doors that led out to a balcony. Stepping out on the balcony, Emily looked out over the backyard. It was a very peaceful setting with its two flower gardens and beautiful birdbath. There were a couple of chairs under a big maple tree. The woods just beyond the yard added to the country feel. Too bad Liz wouldn't be able to realize her dream of making this wonderful old house into a bed and breakfast. Closing the French doors behind her and locking them, Emily glanced around the room before going back downstairs.

How was she going to prove that Liz did not kill herself? With the evidence the police had, she didn't know how she would be able to change Detective Daniels' mind. She had to figure out a way.

As she reached the bottom, Emily suddenly felt totally exhausted. Sitting on the step, she rested her head against the banister. The tears began to flow, and she didn't try to stop them. It looked like she would be spending more than a couple of days in Hampton because she wasn't going to leave until she found out exactly what happened in this house. Someone murdered Liz, and she was going to find out who.

Spotting Liz's mail on the floor by the front door, she decided to put it in her purse and take it with her. She would look through it later to see if there was anything that needed to be taken care of. The grandfather clock in the dining room struck three o'clock as she was getting up. She hadn't realized how late it was. She needed to get back to the Willow Tree so that she could check on the funeral homes in town. Without thinking, she grabbed Liz's purse from the banister and put it on her shoulder.

She let herself out the back door and put those keys in her pocket also. She went through the backyard and made her way to her car. The street was deserted which was a relief for Emily. She didn't want it getting out that she had been at Liz's house, at least not at this time.

Back at the Willow Tree, Maggie handed Emily a note before she could even ask her about funeral homes. The note was from Detective Daniels.

Miss Jansen,

The coroner has sent Miss Marshall's body to Greenbush Funeral Home.

It is the only one in town. You can talk to Mr. Greenbush after 3:30 p.m. If there is anything I can do for you, please let me know.

Detective Daniels.

Realizing that she was carrying two purses, Emily hurried upstairs to avoid any questions from Maggie. Quickly entering the room, she dropped both purses on the chair.

In the bathroom, Emily splashed water on her face and then changed clothes. After combing her hair, she checked herself in the mirror. She was surprised that she looked exactly the same as she had when she arrived in Hampton. She felt like she was a hundred years old. She had to push herself to keep going. With a deep sigh, she turned out the light and went into the bedroom. Picking up her purse, she headed back downstairs to get directions to Greenbush Funeral Home.

"Maggie, could you tell me how to get to Greenbush Funeral Home?"

"It's very simple. Just go to Main Street and take a left. It's just two blocks on the left hand side."

Emily thanked her and went to her car. She really dreaded doing this, but she had no choice. Liz had no family so it was her responsibility to take care of things. The funeral home was easy to find just like Maggie said. Gathering up her courage, she went inside to find Mr. Greenbush.

Walking through a small entryway, Emily came to a bigger room. There was a couch with a couple of chairs, a pedestal that held a book that guests signed, and two separate openings that lead to another area. Stepping through the opening, Emily found herself in the area where the viewing takes place. There were several rows of chairs with an aisle down the middle. The floor slanted downward toward the front of the room almost as if it were a theater instead of a mortuary.

A gentleman came out from behind the curtain that was in the front of the room. He was tall with wavy brown hair that was graying at the temples. The sleeves of his white shirt were rolled up to his elbows. He was also wearing a gray apron. He seemed startled to see her standing there.

"I'm looking for Mr. Greenbush," Emily said clutching her purse. "I'm Emily Jansen. I'm here to discuss Liz Marshall's funeral."

"I'm Mr. Greenbush. Please forgive my appearance. Have a seat, and I will be right with you."

Emily watched him go back behind the curtain. Seeing a chair against the wall behind her she sat down. There was a small table next to the chair with a lamp and a box of tissues on it. Within just a few minutes, Mr. Greenbush was back minus the apron. He had put on a suit jacket making him look more distinguished than he had looked before. Emily stood as he approached.

"Please, Miss Jansen, let's go into my office, and we can begin."

Emily followed him through a doorway she hadn't noticed before to where his office was located. There were two large brown leather chairs in front of a wooden desk. Mr. Greenbush motioned for her to sit in one of the chairs as he went around to sit behind his desk.

"I don't want you to worry about a thing. I can take care of everything for you. Expense is no problem."

"Expense, I hadn't even thought about how I was going to pay for this," Emily said with amazement. "How expensive is a funeral?"

"That is one thing you don't have to worry about Ms Jansen," Mr. Greenbush said, coming around his desk and sitting in the chair next to the one Emily was sitting in. "The expense has been taken care of."

"By whom?"

"Let's just say a friend in town is paying for the funeral." Smiling he patted her arm.

His cold clammy touch sent a shiver up her spine. Moving her arm off the armrest, she asked, "What friend? Who is it so that I can thank him or her?"

"I'm sorry, I can't reveal that information. The person wanted to remain anonymous." Mr. Greenbush reached for a notepad and pen from his desk. "Now let's get started. First, when did you want the funeral to take place? I assume the sooner the better, or did she have family that will be coming in?"

"No, she has no family," Emily remarked quietly.

"Then why don't we schedule it for the day after tomorrow. That will give you one evening for viewing with the public. Which church should I contact, the Catholic Church or the Methodist Church?"

"Liz was Catholic."

"I'll contact Father Jim so that he can set up the mass. Do you want to have it in the morning or the afternoon?"

"It really doesn't make any difference. I suppose in the morning. That's usually when they have most funerals isn't it?"

"Generally, yes, if the church is available. I'll check with Father Jim and see if ten o'clock Thursday would work out for him. What about a luncheon after the funeral?"

"I don't know. Do most people have one?"

"Yes, most do. I can contact the president of the Ladies Guild at the church. They usually serve lunch in the church basement. They take care of everything concerning the luncheon. You don't have to worry about a thing. Since there won't be family in from out of town, it will probably be just a small gathering of friends and neighbors from town. One more thing, Father Jim will conduct a parish wake service tomorrow night. I will make all the arrangements with him."

"That's fine."

Again he patted her arm. She resisted the urge to pull away from him. If he was trying to comfort her, it wasn't working. All she knew was that she wanted this to be over so she could be in the solitude of her room at the Willow Tree.

"Now, Miss Jansen, if you will follow me, we can look at the different types of caskets, and then we can finish the arrangements. I won't be quoting you any prices since everything is taken care of, so you can just pick the one you like best."

Emily followed Mr. Greenbush out of his office and down the aisle in the viewing room. They went through the same curtain he had come through earlier. She was amazed at what she saw. There were about six or seven different caskets to choose from. She decided on a gray casket with mauve colored lining inside.

"Just out of curiosity," Emily remarked. "How much is this one?"

"The price of the casket includes the use of the viewing room, all my services for taking care of the body, the church, plus the burial in the local cemetery." Mr. Greenbush pulled out a card from the inside of the casket and showed it to Emily.

She couldn't believe the price. "I hope the person who agreed to pay for this knows what he's getting into."

"Don't worry. He can afford it," Mr. Greenbush stated flatly. He showed her back to his office where he picked up his pad and pen.

"Do you have anyone you want as pallbearers?"

"I don't know anyone here."

"I'll take care of that for you. We also need to discuss flowers. Usually the family purchases the spray that is put on the casket with a banner that says, "mother," "daughter," " grandmother," etc. What would you like to do?"

"I hadn't thought about flowers. Can you take care of ordering them for me? I guess put "friend" on the banner."

"I would be happy to take care of that for you."

"Is there anything else we need to discuss?" Emily asked hoping they were through.

"I think that should take care of it."

"I really appreciate all your help, Mr. Greenbush. You have been very kind."

"All part of my job, Miss Jansen," Mr. Greenbush said squeezing her arm.

Emily forced herself to smile even though she wanted to run. "I guess I will see you tomorrow. Is there a certain time I should be here?"

"The public viewing will begin about four o'clock. You should be here by about three to see if there is anything that needs to be changed on Miss Marshall before the public comes in."

"Okay, I guess I'll see you about three o'clock tomorrow."

"One more thing. I do need you to bring some clothes for Miss Marshall to wear. If you could bring that by first thing in the morning, I would appreciate it very much."

"I'll get some clothes for you and have them here first thing in the morning." Emily hadn't thought about clothes, but that would give her a legitimate excuse to go back to Liz's house to look around. "Good bye, Mr. Greenbush, and thank you again for all your help."

"Good bye, Miss Jansen," he remarked, bowing slightly.

Emily was relieved to be out in the warm sunshine. The thought of his cold clammy hand touching her sent a shiver up her spine despite the warmth of the sun. She suddenly felt exhausted. She had never planned a funeral before and didn't realize how much planning went into it. When her father had died, she was only about eight years old. She was surprised at how much she actually remembered.

Arriving back at the Willow Tree, Emily was about to go up to her room when she heard someone call her name. Maggie and Detective Daniels were sitting in the dining room drinking a cup of coffee.

"Did you get everything taken care of?" Maggie asked quietly.

"Yes, I did." Emily sat at the table directly across from the detective.

"Would you like some hot tea?" Maggie asked getting up to go into the kitchen.

"Actually, if it's no trouble I would like a glass of iced tea."

"No problem at all. I'll be right back."

Detective Daniels pushed some keys across the table to Emily. "These are the keys to Liz's house."

"Thank you," Emily remarked picking up the keys.

Emily was beginning to feel uneasy sitting across from Daniels. She wanted to be by herself and not have to deal with anyone. Sliding out of the chair, she remarked, "Tell Maggie that I will get the tea later. There's something I have to take care of right now."

Detective Daniels watched her as she hurried out of the room and up the stairs.

"Where's Emily?"

"She took off upstairs."

"What did you say to her to upset her?" Maggie asked sharply.

"I didn't say anything. She just said she had something to take care of and took off."

"Right, I've known you a long time, and you always have a way of shooting off your mouth and antagonizing people. That poor girl has a lot on her plate right now, and she doesn't need you saying something stupid."

"Honest, I didn't say a word." Daniels stood up reaching into his pocket for his keys. "I know when I'm not wanted. I'm out of here."

Maggie just shook her head as he slammed the door on his way out.

Emily let herself drop into the chair next to the door letting her purse fall to the floor. She didn't like Detective Daniels, and she certainly didn't want to try and have a pleasant conversation with him after what she had been through at the funeral home. She knew she hadn't been very nice to Maggie running out before she got back with her tea, but she didn't like being alone in the same room with Daniels.

After kicking off her shoes, Emily stretched out on the bed. She would go downstairs in a little while and talk to Maggie. Right now all she wanted to do was close her eyes and try to relax. The next couple of days were not going to be fun, and she didn't really know what she was going to do after the funeral.

A knock on the door of her room made her jump. She managed to answer, "Yes," as she sat up.

"Emily, this is Maggie, I just wanted to make sure you were all right."

"I'm fine. I'll be down in a little while for that glass of tea."

"Okay, see you in a little bit."

Emily glanced at the floor where her purse had fallen. The contents had spilled everywhere. Sitting on the floor, she began putting things back in her purse. She picked up Liz's mail and began looking through it. Most of it was junk mail, but one envelope caught her eye. The return address was from someone in California. Standing up, she debated whether she should open it or not. She would do that later. Right now she would go down and have that glass of tea.

Emily found her way into the kitchen where Maggie was busy baking. "Sorry I took off earlier. I just needed to be by myself for a little while."

"That's no problem," Maggie remarked setting a glass of iced tea in front of Emily. "I hope Adam, Detective Daniels, didn't say something to offend you."

"No, he didn't say anything."

"You must be hungry. Why don't I fix you a sandwich?"

"That sounds good," Emily replied. "I don't think I've eaten much since breakfast."

Within a short time, Maggie sat a plate in front of her with a sandwich made of ham, cheese, lettuce, and tomato between two pieces of her homemade bread. Also on the plate was a variety of fresh fruit. "Do you expect me to eat all of this?" Emily exclaimed.

"Yes, I do," Maggie, remarked with a chuckle.

At that point, Emily's stomach grumbled making both of them laugh. Picking up the plate, she thanked Maggie for the sandwich and went back to her room.

Emily sat at the desk in the room and munched on her sandwich and fruit. She again went through Liz's mail. Looking at the envelope with the California address, she again wondered if she should open it. Putting her sandwich down, she wiped her hands on her napkin. Using the letter opener that was on the desk, she opened the envelope and took out the letter.

The letter was from a Michael Crawford. He was the brother of Julia Masters, Lee Masters' dead wife. He wanted to talk to Liz about the information she had about Julia's death. He wrote that he was planning on coming to Hampton next week. He thanked Liz for sharing her concerns.

What information did Liz have? She tried to recall her phone conversation with Liz the night before she arrived. Emily couldn't remember anything significant about the conversation. Liz did say she had something she wanted to talk to her about when she got to town. She didn't press her and really didn't think much about it.

Emily looked over the letter again.

Liz,

Thank you for sharing your concerns about Julia's disappearance. I plan on coming to Hampton next week so we can get together and discuss things then. I'm not sure of the exact date, but I will call you when I arrive.

Michael

Michael said he would be coming next week. I guess I'll just have to be in town when he arrives and let him know about Liz. Emily got up from the desk and walked over to the window. Her stay in Hampton would be longer than she thought.

Chapter Three

Emily woke with a start when she felt something cover her mouth. She wasn't sure if this was a part of her dream about Liz, or if it was real. After a couple of seconds passed, she realized she was definitely awake, and someone was in her room with their hand over her mouth. She couldn't scream even though she wanted to. She didn't struggle. She kept very still and tried to make out the dark figure, but was unable to focus.

"Emily, don't make a sound. It's me, Liz."

Now she knew she was still dreaming because Liz was dead. This couldn't possibly be Liz.

"Emily," Liz whispered again. "Wake up and listen to me. I'm going to take my hand away from your mouth, but please don't scream. No one can know that I'm here."

Emily lay very still. It sounded like Liz, but that was impossible. She stayed very still waiting for the person to speak.

"Emily, I'm so sorry to put you through this," Liz said sitting on the bed next to her.

"Can I turn on a light?" Emily whispered.

"Go ahead. The curtains are drawn, so the light shouldn't be a problem."

Emily turned on the light next to the bed. She gasped as she realized this truly was Liz, and she wasn't dead. Emily couldn't help crying as she leaned forward to give Liz a hug.

"I have so many questions," Emily exclaimed as she leaned back in bed. "My mind is trying to take this all in, and I don't know where to begin."

"I'll try to explain as much as I can for now."

"Liz, who was that woman in your bedroom? She looks just like you."

"She is my cousin Tonya."

"You're cousin? I didn't know you had any family left."

"We lost touch when we were kids."

"I can't believe how much she looks like you."

"I know," Liz stated pacing back and forth at the foot of the bed. "It was like looking in a mirror." Liz shivered just thinking about it.

Emily got out of bed and put her arm around Liz. They just stood for a moment not saying anything.

Liz brushed the tears from her cheeks and continued, "Tonya showed up a few days ago. Her mother passed away a couple of months ago, and she decided to do some traveling to work through her feelings."

"Tonya must have been very distraught about her mother to kill herself. Where were you when I came by? Why didn't you call the police? Why are you letting everyone think you're dead? Why did you wait so long to tell me?" She had so many more questions. Her thoughts were in such a jumble. Sitting on the bed, Emily shook her head. "I'm sorry Liz for all the questions. I guess I should give you a chance to answer."

Touching her arm Liz whispered, "I'm sorry Emily. I'll try to explain everything."

Both froze when they heard footsteps outside the door. Looking at each other, they held their breath as they waited for the person to move on. It was only a few seconds, but it seemed like an eternity. When the footsteps faded away, they both let out a sigh of relief.

Liz looked at Emily saying, "I guess the best place to start is at the beginning."

"That would definitely be the place to start," Emily stated sitting cross-legged on the bed and pulling the pillow in front of her.

"Last year I was taking photos at Lee Masters ranch. He didn't mind. But always told me to stay away from one area because he was working with wild horses." Liz got off the bed again and began pacing around the room. "I never thought much about it because there were so many wonderful places to take pictures. One day I was out shooting photos. I heard a small plane flying very low overhead. I looked up to see if I could spot the plane, but the trees were so dense I couldn't see anything." Liz paused and sat down on the bed. "When it sounded like it was landing, I slipped through the woods to see if I could locate it."

Emily was shocked to see Liz look so pale. "Liz," Emily said putting her hand on her arm. "What did you see?"

"I saw Lee Masters and several of his men run out to a small plane that had landed in a clearing. The pilot disembarked, and they stood talking." Liz hesitated, not sure if she wanted to go on.

"Liz, you look frightened. What happened?"

"Lee motioned to someone standing by a small shed. The man brought a woman who had her hands tied and her mouth taped. She was struggling as she was being led. When they reached the plane, the woman continued to struggle, and Lee hit her across the face. After putting her on the plane, Lee handed the pilot an envelope. I can't be sure what was in it, but the pilot looked inside and then shook his head and put the envelope in his pocket. He then got back in the plane and took off."

"Did you recognize the woman?" Emily asked sitting on the bed next to Liz.

"At that time, I couldn't be sure, but I was snapping pictures as fast as I could. When the plane took off, I was so scared that I took off running through the woods back to the little stream where I had my horse tethered." Liz shuddered.

"Did you ever figure out who the woman was that they put on the plane?"

"After I got back to the house, I uploaded those pictures on my computer. From what I could tell, it was Julia Masters whom they forced onto the plane.

"Lee Masters wife?"

"Yes." Liz shivered not from the cold, but from the thought of what Lee had done. "I have been struggling with what to do for about six months now. I kept hoping that Julia would return, and then I wouldn't have to say anything. But Lee just keeps telling the same story that she ran off with a guy she met over the internet."

"You have to go to the police, Liz," Emily remarked drawing her legs up to her chest and putting her arms around them.

"I can't. It is well known in this town that Lee pretty much runs things the way he wants, and the law looks the other way."

"Do you think Lee found out about the pictures?"

"He must have, but I don't know how. I haven't told anyone except you."

Shaking her head, Emily said, "So what does all this have to do with your cousin Tonya committing suicide?"

"Tonya didn't commit suicide Emily; she was murdered."

"How do you know she was murdered?"

"I always go for a walk about seven in the morning, and yesterday was no exception. When I was coming back through the woods, I saw a man walking around to the back of my house. I watched as he went around the side of the house and then crept closer so I could see who it was. I heard voices, and as I looked around the side of the house, I saw a black, four-door, short bed pickup with a silver-racing stripe on the side drive away. When I went inside, I called out for Tonya; but didn't get an answer. I went upstairs to the bedroom and found her."

"Liz, I'm so sorry. Who do you think did it?" Emily got out of bed and put her arm around Liz.

"It was Lee Masters who killed her," Liz replied adamantly.

"How can you be so sure that it was Lee?"

"He is the only person in town who has a pickup like the one I saw. I think he wanted to kill me and mistook Tonya for me."

"Liz, we have to go to the police."

"We can't. If Lee knows I'm alive, he'll just try again to kill me, and the next time he might succeed. He must have found out about the pictures, but how? I didn't tell anyone about them." Liz dropped into the chair next to the door in frustration.

"What about Julia's brother from California?"

"What about him?"

Emily took the letter off the dresser and handed it to Liz. "You received this letter. He said he would be in town next week to talk to you."

Liz read over the letter. "I did send him a note that I was concerned that Julia might not have run off with another man, that something else might have happened to her, but that's all I wrote. There was never any love lost between Michael and Lee, so I can't see Michael saying anything to Lee."

"Are you sure? How else would Lee suspect you?"

"I don't know. I just can't believe that Michael would talk to Lee."

"I hope you're right."

"This letter was written last week, so that means he will be in town sometime this week" Liz remarked looking at the date. "You'll have to meet with him."

"Liz, I don't know if I can do that. What about the funeral?" Emily sat on the edge of the bed and just shook her head.

"You have to keep pretending that I am dead. It's the only way." Liz sat next to Emily and gave her a hug.

"I don't know if I can go through with this. What if I make a mistake, and Lee finds out the truth." Emily looked at Liz with tears in her eyes.

"Listen to me, Emily," Liz remarked. "You can do this. We have to keep up the charade until we can figure things out. Somehow we have to figure out how to prove that Lee is a killer."

"What's this **WE** business? Do you have a mouse in your pocket."

They both started laughing, but quickly put their hands over their mouths so they wouldn't be heard. The laughter helped relieve the tension both of them were feeling.

"There's something else I have to tell you," Emily said looking down at her hands.

"What is it?"

"Detective Daniels said that Lee brought in a suicide note that you sent to him."

"A note? What are you talking about?"

"I guess Lee claims that you sent him a note."

"Why would I send a note to Lee?"

"He claims that you sent him a note telling him why you killed yourself. With the pill bottle and the note from Lee, the police concluded very quickly that you committed suicide."

"Did you see the note?"

"Detective Daniels showed it to me. It told Lee that you

couldn't live with yourself anymore because of what you did to Julia."

"What I did to Julia? What are you talking about?"

"According to the note, you confessed to killing Julia and that you killed yourself out of guilt."

"So Lee is trying to pin Julia's death on me to cover up what he did to both Julia and Tonya."

"Do you have the pictures with you?"

"No, I have them safely hidden in the house. It's amazing how many little nooks and crannies there are in old houses."

"Do you think Lee had time to look for them?"

"I don't know. He made sure everything was very neat and tidy. He didn't leave anything out of place." Liz chewed on her thumb trying to calm her nerves. "I checked the hiding place, and the pictures were still there."

"Do you think he'll come back to look for them again?"

"I don't know, but I wouldn't put anything past him."

"My gosh, Liz," Emily remarked kneeling up on the bed. "Where have you been staying? Have you been at the house?"

"I've been staying in the attic over the garage. It's not very comfortable, but I feel pretty safe there. I hid in the woods until it got dark and then sneaked into the garage and up to the attic. There are a lot of places to hide in the house also, but I really didn't want to do that in case Lee came back. Also, the thought of what happened there kind of unnerved me."

"I got there just shortly after this all happened. I felt sick when I saw you lying there or should I say Tonya." Emily pulled the pillow closer to her wishing that vision of Tonya would just go away.

"I'm sorry Emily." Liz got up from the chair and sat on the bed next to Emily. "I thought about waiting for you so I could explain everything to you, but I didn't want to chance Lee coming back and finding me there."

"I know you couldn't tell me then because it was too dangerous. I understand."

"Since the police are through at the house, you can come and go as you like. No one will think anything of it. You need to keep an eye on those pictures until we can figure out what to do. I've hidden them on the third floor in the turret room at the front of the house. There is a hidden drawer along the wall opposite the window. Just run your hand along the molding, and you will discover it."

"How did you know it was there?"

"I discovered it quite by accident when I was cleaning in that room shortly after I moved in." Liz looked at the clock on the nightstand and realized how late it was or actually how early it was. "Oh my, it's almost four o'clock. I have to get going." Liz remarked getting up from the bed.

"By the way, how did you get in here in the first place?" Emily asked looking around the room.

"Through there," Liz remarked pointing to the window. "And up the trellis."

"You're braver than I am. Come to think of it, how did you know that I was here?"

"This is the only decent place to stay, and besides, I've been keeping my eye on you."

"I'm glad you have. One more thing," Emily remarked touching Liz's arm. "You knew where I might be staying, but how did you know which room?

"When I was watching last night, I saw you open the curtains and open the window."

"Very clever of you."

They gave each other a long hug and then Liz slipped out the window and down the trellis. Keeping in the shadows so she wouldn't be detected, she continued the few blocks to her house and slipped through a side door in the garage and up to the attic.

Emily crawled back into bed after Liz left and turned out the light. Shivering more from what she had just learned rather than from being cold, she pulled the covers close around her trying to feel safe. The next two days were going to be very trying. She knew she had to do this for Liz, so somehow she would find the strength she needed to pull this off. There was no way she was going to let Lee know that Liz was alive and that he had killed the wrong person.

Once the funeral was over, she and Liz could figure out how to convince the police that Lee was the killer of both Tonya and Julia. Somehow they had to find a way to bring Lee to justice. They had to do it for Tonya and Julia.

The clock showed almost four-thirty. She needed to get some sleep, but things were just spinning around in her head. Tomorrow and the next day were going to be very trying, and she would need her wits about her. Finally Emily turned on her side and curled up in a ball pulling the cover around her. Taking a couple of deep breaths, she tried to relax her body and clear her mind so that she could finally fall asleep.

Emily looked at the clock. It was only 6:00 a.m. It surprised her to be awake so early after the late night talking to Liz. She decided to take a quick shower and have some breakfast before going over to Liz's to pick out an outfit to take to the mortuary. Knowing Liz was alive made things a little easier, but it would still be stressful getting through the public viewing and the funeral.

The smell of bacon and coffee pierced Emily's senses as soon as she opened her door. She couldn't help but smile as she made her way downstairs to the dining room. Her stomach growled rather loudly as she walked into the room. Emily was relieved that no one else was there.

The sideboard was full of breakfast delights. There was so much to choose from, scrambled eggs, bacon, sausage, biscuits, cinnamon rolls, toast, waffles, and a variety of fresh fruit. Also, besides coffee and hot tea, Maggie had prepared a variety of juices.

"Good morning," Maggie said cheerfully as she came into the dining room. "I hope you had a good night's sleep. I am surprised that you are up already."

"I'm surprised myself. Maybe it was the thought of all this wonderful food down here that made me want to get up early."

"You just help yourself and enjoy."

Emily was so busy helping herself to the veritable smorgasbord of delicious breakfast items that she didn't hear Jack Baker come up beside her. She almost bumped into him as she turned to take a seat at the table. Jack caught her arm and took hold of her plate to keep it from falling. Emily's cheeks became a bright red as she tried to apologize for the near mishap. "I'm terribly sorry, Mr. Baker. Are you okay?"

"I'm fine. I should be apologizing to you for not letting you know I was so close." Jack took the plate from Emily and put it on the table. "Are you okay, Miss Jansen?"

"I'm fine." Sitting at the table, Emily tried to compose herself. She didn't understand why she felt so flustered.

Jack put his plate on the table across from Emily. "Would you like something to drink?"

Emily put her napkin up to her mouth and quickly tried to swallow her food before answering. She did manage to shake her head "yes" as she swallowed. "A glass of orange juice would be nice, thank you."

Jack filled two glasses with juice and gave one to Emily.

"Thank you, Mr. Baker." Emily looked at Jack quizzically as he turned and looked around the room.

"Sorry, I thought my father was here. Please, call me Jack. My father was always Mr. Baker," Jack said with a wink.

Emily remarked with a smile, "And you may call me Emily." Laughing, Emily said, "I think we had this conversation once before."

Jack nodded, "We did." He sunk his teeth into a huge

cinnamon roll. "Mmmm, this is delicious. You should try one, Emily."

"I saw them, but there are just too many things to choose. I don't have room for everything."

"They certainly are good," Jack remarked taking another big bite.

"I thought about sneaking one up to my room for later," Emily whispered.

Who's sneaking what up to their room?" Maggie asked as she walked into the dining room.

Both Emily and Jack just shrugged their shoulders.

"Well, I think I better just keep an eye on my precious silver to make sure none of it disappears." Maggie chuckled as she checked on the food.

"Why don't you sit down and join us," Emily suggested. "There are no other guests right now, and the food is just fine."

"That's a good idea," Jack added.

"Okay, but just for a quick cup of coffee and then it's back to the kitchen." Maggie poured herself a cup and sat at the table. "I don't suppose either of you would like to help me in the kitchen this morning."

"I would love to, but I have a million things that I have to do this morning. Maybe Jack is able to help you." Emily grinned at Jack watching him come up with some kind of excuse.

"Actually, I have a couple of pressing appointments to take care of this morning. Otherwise, Maggie, I would love to help you."

"Sure, sure. Everyone always has an excuse."

Emily couldn't help but laugh at the playful exchange. It felt so good to be able to forget about the matter at hand even for a short while.

"If you two will excuse me, I have some business to take

care of. You both have a good day." Emily left the dining room and hurried up the stairs to get her purse. The first order of business was to find an outfit for Liz to wear in the casket. Except, thank goodness, it wasn't Liz. She felt bad for Liz's cousin, but was so glad that Liz was fine.

Grabbing her purse off the chair she headed back out the door and down the steps. Out in the sunlight Emily took a deep breath. She loved this time of the morning. The sun was just beginning to dry the dew on the grass and warm the early morning air. A light breeze brushed gently against her face.

Rolling down the window on her car, Emily enjoyed the fresh morning air on her short drive to Liz's. If she didn't have to go to the funeral home when she was finished at Liz's, she would have walked to help clear her head. Pulling into the driveway, she just sat contemplating everything that had transpired since her arrival in Hampton. It was like she was living a dream, and she kept hoping that she wouldn't have to continue with this charade.

After unlocking the door, Emily stepped into the cool darkness of the entry. She laid the keys on the table by the door and just stood looking around. Walking into the living room, she opened the curtains letting the light spill into the room. With the wraparound porch the sun never shone directly into the room, but the light from outside helped brighten the room making Emily feel better about being in the house.

She headed up the stairs to Liz's room to find an outfit for Liz, aka Tonya, to wear. At the top of the stairs, she hesitated about going up to the third floor now or wait until she was finished picking out an outfit. The pictures could wait. She wanted to accomplish the grim task of which outfit to choose first.

Emily went into Liz's room and opened her closet. "I should have asked Liz what outfit to get for Tonya." The sound of her voice startled her. She hadn't realized that she had spoken out loud. She froze with her hand in midair when she thought she heard a door close. Should she investigate or just pretend she didn't hear anything.

"Hello, is anyone here?"

Emily slowly exhaled when she heard a woman's voice. She couldn't imagine who it might be, but at least it wasn't someone trying to sneak around the house.

"Hello," the voice called again.

Finding her own voice, Emily replied, "I'll be right down."

Hurrying out of the room, Emily made sure to close the door to the bedroom. She went downstairs to find the person connected with the voice. What she found was a short, dark-haired rather plump woman snooping through the things Liz had on her bookshelf in her living room.

"May I help you?" Emily asked, annoyed at the woman's brash behavior.

The woman turned quickly at the sound of Emily's voice. "Oh, hello."

"May I help you with something?"

"I'm Jennifer Brack from next door." She extended her hand to shake Emily's and quickly pulled it back when she realized she was holding a statue. She put the statue back on the shelf and cleared her throat to gain her composure.

"Is there something I can do for you?" Emily remarked trying hard not to grin.

"Oh my, no. I saw the car in the driveway and the curtains open and was just wondering who might be in Liz's house. I didn't want anyone to be snooping around and taking things they shouldn't.

"Thank you for being concerned. I'm a friend of Liz's and, unfortunately, I am handling her funeral arrangements. While I'm in town, I will be checking on the house.

"That is such a great comfort to me," Jennifer remarked with a deep sigh and putting her hand on her chest. "Liz and I were friends, and it's nice to know that she has someone to take care of things in this terrible situation."

Emily put her hand over her mouth and cleared her throat to avoid laughing. She remembered Liz talking about her nosey neighbor. She couldn't remember the name Liz said, but she had to be the one. Emily took Jennifer by the arm and walked with her toward the door. "Thank you so much for your concern. I know Liz would have appreciated your looking out for her." Opening the door, Emily continued, "It was nice meeting you Jennifer. You have a nice day." Jennifer opened her mouth to speak, but Emily closed and locked the door before she could say anything.

"Now that I'm rid of that busybody, back to the matter at hand." Emily went back to Liz's bedroom to find an outfit.

She pulled a beige outfit from the back of her closet and decided to take it. Liz would need her clothes when this was all over with, and she didn't want to take anything that she might still wear. Something from the back of the closet would be safer to take since it probably wasn't worn much any more.

After checking the time, Emily decided to take the outfit over to the funeral home and then come back to look for the pictures. She wouldn't have to rush when she came back.

Parking her car in front of the funeral home, Emily picked up the outfit and went inside. The coolness of the entry made her shiver. She was not looking forward to the viewing and the funeral tomorrow. The only thing that made this all bearable was that Liz was alive.

"Good morning, Miss Jansen," Mr. Greenbush said coming out of his office.

"Good morning." Emily shivered again when his hand touched hers as she handed him the outfit. She really didn't like Mr. Greenbush. He had been very helpful and kind, but there was just something about him.

"Thank you very much. This should do nicely. I will see you about three o'clock this afternoon."

"I will be here. Thank you."

Emily stepped outside and enjoyed the warmth of the sun.

After getting into her car, she realized that she should check the clothes she brought along to make sure she had appropriate outfits for today and tomorrow. She hadn't planned on attending a funeral. The clock in her car read 9:30, so she had plenty of time to go back to Liz's and check out the information before planning her wardrobe.

I hope Jennifer Brack doesn't decide to come back over for a visit when she sees my car in the driveway again. Emily let herself into the house and locked the door behind her. That should at least keep her out until I decide to answer the door if she would come by.

Quickly ascending the stairs to the third floor, she found the turret room in the front of the house. It took a few seconds for Emily's eyes to adjust to the dimness of the room. With her hand, she began feeling over the chair rail on the wall without a window.

She had just about given up when her hand hit a small knob beneath the chair rail. Pressing the knob, the drawer popped open. Before taking the envelope out of the drawer, Emily went to the window to make sure no one was coming, and she listened to make sure she didn't hear the doorbell.

Reassured that she was completely alone, Emily took the envelope out of the drawer. She pulled the lone chair over by the window. After settling in the chair, she took the contents out of the envelope. There were several pictures. Liz had enlarged the photos, and Emily could clearly see the faces of the people in the pictures. She had met Lee and Julia only once, but if Lee was the person she saw at the police station, then Lee was definitely the person hitting the woman in the picture. You could see that she was struggling as the men led her to the plane. The pictures played out a frightening scenario.

She could see why Lee wanted this information and why he would kill to get it. Taking a deep sigh, Emily carefully placed the pictures back in the envelope. She would have to be very careful especially if he had been the one to pay for the funeral. Putting the envelope back in the drawer and closing it, Emily rested her head against the wall. She was terrified by what she had just seen, but she had to pull herself together for Liz. Together they had to expose Lee for what he really was, a cold-blooded killer.

At the Willow Tree Inn, Emily looked through the clothes hanging in the closet. She came to the conclusion that she would definitely need something for tomorrow. She had a black pair of pants and a long sleeved white blouse that would be appropriate for today, but she didn't have anything that would do for tomorrow. Maybe she could find a black skirt with a lightweight jacket. She would ask Maggie for suggestions as to where to shop.

Maggie was sitting at the dining room table folding napkins when Emily came down. "Hi," she remarked, sitting down across from Maggie.

"Hi, did you get all your business taken care of?"

"Almost. I've discovered that I need something to wear tomorrow for the funeral. I was hoping that you could suggest a dress shop for me."

"There isn't a lot to choose from. Were you looking for something basic?"

"Yes, just a simple black skirt with maybe a lightweight jacket, nothing fancy."

"I would suggest Annie's Dress Shop. They have the basics, and they aren't too expensive. They're right on Main Street, so you shouldn't have any trouble finding them."

"Thanks, I'll see you later."

Maggie was right, Emily thought as she put her packages into the car. Annie's had been a good place to shop. She found a black skirt and also a cream colored blouse to go with it. To top it off, she had found a short, lightweight jacket.

Looking at her watch, Emily figured she had just enough time to grab a sandwich and then head back to the inn to change before going to the funeral home.

Emily found a café just around the corner from the dress

shop. It was the same one she had been to on Monday. Hopefully there weren't a lot of people inside, and the conversations were about something other than Liz. She went inside and sat in a booth. Leaning back, she tried to relax and build up her courage for what was ahead.

"How are you today?" the waitress asked with a smile.

"I'm fine, thank you."

"Can I get you something to drink?"

"Water with no lemon, please."

"Here's the menu, and I'll be right back with your water."

"Thank you."

Emily looked over the menu and decided on a club sandwich. The waitress brought her water and set it on the table in front of her.

"Were you ready to order, or did you need a few more minutes?"

"I'm ready. I'll have the club sandwich, and can I substitute a side salad instead of fries?"

"Yes, you can. What kind of dressing would you like?"

"You know, on second thought I think I'll just have the fries."

"No problem," the waitress remarked scratching out the salad and writing down fries.

Emily leaned her head back against the seat. The coolness of the leather felt good against the back of her head. Closing her eyes, she tried to put everything that had happened the last few days into perspective. This was not what she had planned when she decided to visit Liz for the summer. What a crazy, crazy world it was.

"Here you are, ma'am." The waitress placed the food in front of Emily and with a smile turned to leave.

"Thank you," Emily replied.

The club sandwich was very good, just the way she liked it. She was surprised at how hungry she was after having such a big breakfast, but that had been very early this morning. After paying her bill, Emily went back to the inn to get ready to go to the funeral home.

Chapter Four

After parking her car, Emily just sat with her hands on the steering wheel. She didn't want to do this, but she knew she didn't have a choice in the matter. Resting her head on the steering wheel, she closed her eyes and said a quick prayer. Liz was alive and she was very grateful for that, but she didn't want to sit and listen to people talking about Liz in the past tense. It was going to be very hard pretending that it was Liz in the casket and not her cousin Tonya. Looking at her watch Emily knew it was time to go inside. The sooner she got started, the sooner the whole ordeal would be over.

The sun felt good as she stepped out of the car. Emily closed her eyes and tried to drink in its warmth. The mortuary would be cool and overbearing. The warmth from the sun would have to last her a few hours. Standing in the entry, Emily felt the place did not seem peaceful and serene. There was something about it and Mr. Greenbush that put her on edge.

Emily pasted an expressionless look on her face and entered the viewing room. Mr. Greenbush was standing by the casket arranging the flowers.

"Good afternoon, Mr. Greenbush," Emily managed to say quietly.

"Good afternoon, Miss Jansen. I know this isn't easy for you, but if you would come forward and take a look at your friend, I would like to know if everything is to your satisfaction. I can change the hair and the makeup but nothing else."

Emily slowly stepped toward the casket. She knew it wasn't Liz in there, but she still didn't want to look at her double. Gazing into the casket Emily covered her mouth with her hand, and tears welled in her eyes. She searched her face to get some kind of distinguishing feature that showed this was Tonya and not Liz. Without seeing her eyes there was no way anyone could tell the difference. Lee would never know he killed the wrong person.

"I'm sorry, Miss Jansen. I do have to ask if you find everything satisfactory." Mr. Greenbush touched her arm as he spoke and handed her a tissue.

"Yes, everything is fine, Mr. Greenbush. She looks fine." Emily dabbed her eyes with the tissue continuing, "Thank you for doing such a fine job." She could not help but think that everything was not fine. Liz wasn't fine, Tonya wasn't fine, and she wasn't fine. Hearing Mr. Greenbush's voice brought her back to the task at hand.

"I'm glad you approve. Before people begin arriving, I'd like to go over a few things with you."

"Okay."

"Why don't we sit over here," Mr. Greenbush said indicating a couch just a few feet away.

"Thank you," Emily mumbled, not knowing what else to say.

"First the ladies' room is right down the hall to your right. After a couple of hours, I will come and see if you would like to take a break and sit in the lounge or get a breath of fresh air. In the lounge we have coffee, tea, or water to drink. There are also some cookies to munch on. If I see that you are getting a little overwhelmed before this, I will come out and give you a break before the two hours is up. Do you have any questions?"

Emily was surprised at his concern, but then remembering what this funeral cost, she knew that it was not genuine and that he was just doing his job. "I don't think I have any questions. Do I have time to use the ladies' room?"

"Yes, go right ahead."

Leaning against the door of the ladies' room, Emily took a deep breath. She knew she had to do this for Liz. It was just a few hours, and she would manage to get through it. Looking at her watch, she saw that it was almost four o'clock. Placing her purse on the counter, Emily combed her hair and touched up her makeup. "Show time," she said taking one last look in the mirror.

Mr. Greenbush was not in the viewing room when she came back. Emily took her seat on the couch and tucked her purse next to her. She was as ready as she'd ever be.

A man dressed in black dress pants and a white long sleeved western style shirt and black cowboy boots was the first to arrive. He walked up to the casket and paused a moment before turning and looking at Emily. She had seen him before. He was the man at the police station when she had gone in to talk to Detective Daniels. He was also the man in the pictures that she had looked at earlier that day. So this was Lee Masters. He was very good looking with his brown wavy hair and tan face. She could tell by the way he walked toward her that he thought he owned the world.

"I'm very sorry for the loss of your friend. I'm sure you don't remember me. We met several years ago when you and Liz came out to my ranch. I'm Lee Masters. Liz and I were friends for a long time."

"I do remember Liz mentioning your name. I also remember seeing you at the police station the other day." He stood looking down on her like he was the king and she was just a lowly peon. Wasn't it appropriate that the cowboy hat he held in his hands was black?

"I was down at the police station because I wanted to give them the note I received in the mail. I'm sure Detective Daniels showed it to you."

"Yes, he showed it to me. I found it quite interesting and unfortunately it gave me the answers to several questions I had about Liz's death." Was he fishing to find out if she agreed Liz committed suicide? She wasn't about to let on that she thought any differently, not at this time anyway. "I was very surprised because I never figured Liz could do something like that. I guess you really never know someone." That seemed to be what he wanted to hear.

He nodded his head in agreement. "It seems like you never really know someone even though they are close to you." He picked up her hand and held it, staring at her the whole time.

Emily pulled her hand away and said quietly, "Thank you for coming."

Before Lee could comment further, Jennifer Brack sat down next to Emily and began dabbing her eyes with a tissue. "Oh, my dear, this is just terrible. Liz was such a nice person. I can't imagine her doing something like this. This must be just terrible for you coming here for a visit and finding her body. How are you holding up? This is just terrible." She picked up Emily's hand and held it between her own. Shaking her head, she continued to ramble. "I feel responsible for this. I should have seen the signs and stopped her."

Emily just looked at her in amazement. Liz couldn't stand Jennifer and hardly said two words to her when they would meet. She considered her a busybody. Now all of a sudden, according to Jennifer, she and Liz were great friends. She continued talking, but Emily just tuned her out.

"Jennifer, do you mind if I talk to Emily for a minute?"

Emily looked up to see Maggie standing there. Jennifer just glared at her, but got up so Maggie could sit down.

"We can talk some more later," Jennifer stated walking off in a huff.

"You looked like you needed rescuing."

"Thank you so much for that. She is a real nuisance."

"People cross the street just to avoid her when they see her coming."

"I believe that."

"How are you holding up?"

"I'm doing okay."

"This whole thing can't be easy for you." Maggie patted Emily on the arm.

"Not quite what I expected to be doing when I came to visit," Emily said taking a tissue and dabbing her eyes.

"I should let you go."

"Oh, please, Maggie, could you sit with me for a little while? I could certainly use a little moral support."

"I can stay for a while."

Emily was surprised at the number of people who came to the wake. Liz must have been well known in town. Maggie told her who the curiosity seekers were, especially since Liz's death was labeled a suicide.

"Do you think it would be terrible of me to sneak off to the restroom?" Emily asked Maggie. "I'm beginning to feel a little overwhelmed, and I need to gain my composure before the parish wake service starts."

"I'm sure it's just fine," Maggie replied with a smile.

"Thanks. I'll be right back." Emily hurried out of the room and down a hallway to the ladies room.

She closed the door and breathed a sigh of relief to be alone. Looking in the mirror, Emily combed her hair and touched up her lipstick. This whole charade was more difficult than she imagined. It was very hard to just sit there and not shout out that the person in the casket wasn't Liz. Her knowing that was the only thing that made the wake bearable. With one last look in the mirror, she went out the door and back to her seat.

"Feel better?"

"Yes, I do. I think I can make it through the rest of the evening." Emily tucked her purse next to her on the couch. More people were filing past the casket, and the chairs were beginning to fill up. Emily just smiled and nodded every time someone expressed his or her condolences.

"I can't believe how many people are here," Emily whispered to Maggie. "I realize it is a small town, and everybody knows everybody, but I never expected anything like this."

"A lot of the members of the parish come out for the parish service even if they didn't know the person that well," Maggie explained to Emily.

"That explains all the people. I know Liz got along with everybody."

"Excuse me, Miss Jansen, this is Father Jim." After the introduction, Mr. Greenbush hurried off to hand out booklets to everyone.

"I am very sorry for your loss, Miss Jansen. After the service I would like to visit with you for a few minutes if I may," Father Jim remarked shaking Emily's hand.

"That would be just fine."

Following along in the booklet that she was given, Emily thought back to her father's wake service. She was only eight years old at the time, but she remembered all the things people said about her dad. Her dad had been very active in the church and a very giving person. The funeral home was overflowing with people who had come to pay their respects. Sitting there listening to all those people, she couldn't understand why God would take him away. She had been angry with Him for a long time.

Emily's attention was drawn back to the present when Father Jim asked if anyone had anything they would like to say about Liz. One by one people got up and told how Liz had touched their lives. Tears streamed down her face as she listened. She recognized the voice of the last person to speak. It was Lee Masters. He spoke of how much he respected Liz and how much he had learned from her.

Emily just wanted to turn around and tell him to shut up, but she controlled herself. He was such a hypocrite and would soon be exposed for the evil person he was.

Father Jim read the closing prayers from the booklet and sprinkled holy water on the body. He came over to the couch to visit with Emily. Maggie moved over so that he could sit next to her.

"Thank you for a very beautiful service. I know Liz would have loved it."

"She was a very special person. We are going to miss her. She had a way about her so that everyone would just follow her lead. She was able to defuse many an argument."

"She was always like that, even in school."

"I wanted to ask you if there were any particular music that you wanted the choir to sing tomorrow."

"Oh my, I hadn't really thought about that." After a moment Emily shook her head. "No, not really. I'll leave that up to you and the choir."

"Fine. I will see you tomorrow." With that, Father Jim made his way to the back of the room and out the door.

Emily looked at her watch. It was almost seven thirty, so there was only about a half hour left. Eight o'clock couldn't get here soon enough. A couple more people came up to view the body and offer their condolences. She was surprised to see Jack Baker there.

"I really am sorry about your friend," Jack said after going up to the casket. "If there's anything you need or something I can help with, don't hesitate to ask."

"Thank you," Emily said quietly.

Jack didn't say any more and said his good-byes.

There were just a few people left. It was almost eight o'clock when Detective Daniels came in. He walked up to the casket and stood silently for a moment and then came over to where Emily and Maggie were sitting. "I really am sorry about all of this. If there is anything I can do, please let me know."

"Thank you." Emily really wanted to say more, but now was not the time or the place. She would say plenty when the time was right.

Finally it was time to leave. Maggie left to go back to the inn while Emily talked to Mr. Greenbush. He told her what time she needed to be at the mortuary in the morning, and then she left to go back to the inn.

Leaning back against the seat of her car, Emily felt totally drained. It had only been four hours, but it seemed like an eternity. All she wanted to do was go back to the inn and go to bed.

Maggie and Jack were both in the living room when she arrived. "I know you're probably exhausted," Maggie remarked when she came in, "but why don't you join us for a few minutes. I'll make a cup of chamomile tea to help you relax."

Emily was too tired to argue. She nodded yes and sat down in a flowered Queen Anne chair. Maggie brought her the tea and set it on the table next to her. Picking up the teacup, Emily took a sip. Closing her eyes and leaning her head back against the chair she let the warmth of the tea flow down her throat.

"Thank you. That is just what I needed." Emily slipped out of her shoes and rubbed her feet on the carpet. "I never knew that sitting could be so exhausting."

"This isn't a very relaxing situation for you," Jack stated taking a sip of his tea. "I'm sure this wasn't what you had planned when you came to see your friend."

"No, it wasn't. We were going to have such a great time this summer. I was going to help her fix up the Victorian house she had bought. It had been such a long time since we were able to spend any time together. Our schedules just never seemed to allow it. We did manage to talk on the phone at least once or twice a week." Taking another sip of her tea, she swallowed slowly to allow the tea to relax her as it went down.

"Despite your distance apart, you still maintained a close relationship." Maggie said refilling Emily's teacup and then offering more to Jack who shook his head.

"We were friends since grade school. We always managed to keep in touch no matter how busy our schedules were or what we were doing. Our friendship was very important to both of us." Sighing deeply, Emily shook her head. "It's just hard to comprehend everything that has happened the last few days." Tears came even though she tried to prevent them. Maggie offered her a tissue, which she gratefully accepted.

"I have a favor to ask of you, Maggie. I know we just met, and that you are very busy running this bed and breakfast, but would you go with me in the morning to the funeral home and then to church. I really don't want to go by myself. I will if I have to, and I do understand if you say 'no'." Emily gave Maggie a pleading look hoping she would say yes.

"Of course, I will. I know this is a very difficult situation, and it makes things worse when you have to handle everything by yourself."

"Thank you. I really appreciate your kindness."

"Here is one of Liz's memorial cards. I picked one up for you."

"I didn't even think about getting one." Reading over the card, she was surprised to see Lee's name as one of the pallbearers. "Who are the pallbearers? I only recognize Lee Masters name."

"I believe the others are men from her church. I think that's what I heard tonight."

"Lee Masters' name seems to be turning up a lot."

"He is a very powerful man."

He wants to make sure Liz is put in the ground so that she can't tell the police what actually happened to her. Boy, is he in for a surprise, Emily thought.

"I think I'll head upstairs. Mr. Greenbush said we should be there around nine o'clock. I know I'll be up and ready long before that. See you in the morning."

"Good night," Maggie and Jack said as they watched Emily go up to her room.

"She's holding up quite well despite all that has happened. It's no fun to have to go through something like this by yourself."

"You sound like you're talking from experience," Maggie said picking up the teacups.

"Unfortunately, I am." Jack didn't elaborate, and Maggie didn't pry.

"I just hope she comes to accept the fact that her friend killed herself. It will definitely make things harder if she can't."

"What makes you think that she won't?" Jack asked, taking the teapot back to the kitchen.

"She told me that she doesn't think her friend committed suicide. She said that Liz hated sleeping pills because her father had killed himself by taking them. She doesn't think there is any way that Liz could have taken a bottle of sleeping pills."

"Oh really," Jack stated, becoming very curious. "Did she tell this to the police?"

"She said that she did and they just dismissed it. Detective Daniels himself said that it was suicide, and that they weren't investigating any further."

"Interesting. Well, good night. I'll see you in the morning."

Chapter Five

Maggie and Jack were already in the dining room when Emily came downstairs. "Good morning," the two said in unison.

"There's coffee and hot tea on the sideboard. Would you like me to make some breakfast before we go?" Maggie asked wiping her hands on her apron.

"No, thank you. I'll just have some toast and hot tea. I don't think I could eat a big breakfast." Emily put a teabag in her cup and poured the hot water over it. Picking up her cup, she took a piece of toast and sat down at the table.

"I'm so grateful that you are going with me, Maggie. I just didn't want to face the funeral alone."

"I'm glad to help. I didn't know Liz very will, but she was always very friendly and pleasant when we did talk."

Sipping on the tea helped to calm Emily's nerves. After a couple bites of toast she couldn't eat any more. Her stomach was in knots. "I guess its time to go," she remarked, looking at the grandfather clock that stood in the corner of the dining room.

"Why don't you ride with me, Emily," Maggie said, grabbing her purse. "You have enough on your mind."

"Actually, why don't I play chauffer?" Jack said getting up from the table.

Emily was surprised by the offer and was about to object when Maggie commented, "That's very nice of you, Jack, but you really don't have to do this."

"I know I don't, but I want to. I know this isn't easy for you, and I would just like to help. Shall we ladies?" Jack said opening the door. "Your chariot awaits."

As they pulled up to the funeral home, a man came up to the car and instructed Jack on where to park for the funeral procession. Jack stayed with the car while Emily and Maggie went inside.

After viewing the body, they sat on the couch to wait. Since Liz had no family, there were only a few people who came to the funeral home before the mass.

The pallbearers were off to the side in a little alcove talking quietly. Emily noticed Lee with them. He seemed to know all of them from the way he talked to them. He looked around, and when he noticed Emily looking his way, he flashed her a big smile. She felt her cheeks get warm as she blushed. She quickly looked away.

Mr. Greenbush led them past the casket one more time and then they went out to Jack's car. They sat in the car and watched as the pallbearers brought out the casket and placed it in the hearse. The pallbearers then got into a white limousine behind the hearse.

It was a short procession to the church where Father Jim was waiting for them. After saying a few prayers, he led the procession down the aisle to the front of the church. Emily was shocked when Jennifer Brack got behind them as they started down the aisle. I guess she considered herself a good friend of

Liz's. The choir sang many songs familiar to Emily. Both Father Jim and the choir did a wonderful job. After the closing prayer was read, the priest and the servers stood in front of the casket sprinkling holy water and incense. The pallbearers again led the procession out of church.

They drove in silence to the cemetery. Emily just looked out the window not really seeing anything. She brushed a stray tear from her cheek. Even knowing that it wasn't Liz didn't make it any easier going through the funeral. Emily wondered what Liz was doing right now knowing that it was supposed to have been her in the casket. The slowing of Jack's car caused Emily to look up. They were turning into the cemetery and driving up to the location of the grave. She couldn't wait for this to be over, actually for the entire day to be over.

Maggie reached over and patted Emily's hand.

Emily gave her a weak smile. "I will be so glad when I'm back at the Willow Tree and have peace and quiet."

The car came to a stop, and Mr. Greenbush and his helper came to open the car doors for Emily and Maggie. Stepping out of the car, they waited for the casket to be taken from the hearse. They followed behind the pallbearers to the gravesite. There were several chairs set up by the casket. Mr. Greenbush led Emily to the first chair, and Maggie sat next to her. There was one empty chair left and Jennifer Brack took it upon herself to sit there. The rest of the people crowded in behind the chairs. Jack stayed back at the car.

Father Jim read from his prayer book and then sprinkled the casket with holy water. After he was finished, he handed the crucifix that was on the casket to Emily. Father Jim handed the holy water to Mr. Greenbush. He in turn helped Emily from her seat and handed it to her. She sprinkled the casket and then handed it back to Mr. Greenbush. There were several roses in the spray of flowers on the casket, and Mr. Greenbush handed one to Emily. In turn he did the same with Maggie and Jennifer Brack. When they were all finished, they went back to the car.

Jennifer Brack was hurrying to their car, but Jack

intercepted her. He said something to her quietly, and then she turned and left.

As they were driving out of the cemetery, Emily noticed a woman standing all by herself at the edge of the cemetery. She was dressed all in black and was wearing a big black hat and sunglasses. She didn't move from her spot, but stood watching.

"I wonder who that lady is?" Emily remarked. "She is just standing there by herself."

"Maybe it's someone who knew Liz as an acquaintance, but didn't want to intrude. Unlike Jennifer Brack," Maggie said, shaking her head.

"She really had some nerve. I'm sure she will be right with us at the luncheon also. Not wanting to miss out on anything."

"She does add a little comic relief to the whole situation," Jack said with a chuckle.

"That she does," Emily agreed. "That she does."

"Aren't you headed in the wrong direction? The church is the other way." Maggie asked Jack as he turned right instead of left.

"I figured I'd take the long way around to the church. You don't mind a little more time without a crowd of people to contend with, do you, Emily?" Jack flashed her a mischievous smile.

Emily couldn't help but grin. "I don't mind at all, not at all."

"Sometimes, Jack, you do come up with good ideas."

"What do you mean sometimes, Maggie? I'm full of good ideas."

The hills were so green and beautiful. It made a wonderful pastoral scene with the cattle and horses grazing. There was a tractor working in a field making big round hay bales. As they drove a little farther, they passed a big two-story farmhouse. The house was white with dark gray shutters. A big red barn sat a short distance from the house. A white fence enclosed the entire farmstead. The lawn and trees surrounding the house were very neat. You could tell that the people who lived there took great pride in what they had. The view was very relaxing.

Jack turned down a white chalk road that rolled along with the hills. The motion of the car going up and down the hills was very enjoyable.

"I could pick up a little speed and drive these hills faster if you two were so inclined." He pressed a little harder on the gas pedal just to see what type of reaction he would get.

"You don't have to speed up," Maggie remarked trying to sound upset. "We want to get back to town in one piece."

"You're just no fun." Jack let up on the gas pedal and resumed the slower speed. He looked in his rearview mirror to see how Emily was doing. She seemed to be enjoying the peacefulness of the countryside. Too bad they had to get back for the luncheon.

All too soon for Emily, they headed back to town. She needed this little diversion and felt she could face the people for another couple of hours. At least then she could move on to the important business of proving Lee guilty of Julia's murder and also Tonya's.

Before they could get out of the car at the church Jennifer Brack came running up to them, "Where have you been? Everybody has been waiting for you."

"It's okay, Jennifer. I told Mr. Greenbush that we had an errand to run and would be here as quickly as possible. He didn't have a problem with that." Jack took Jennifer by the arm and escorted her to the church basement.

"Jack has been so wonderful the last two days. He has helped out so much. Not everyone would do that for a complete stranger. And you, Maggie," Emily said squeezing her arm. "You have been absolutely fantastic. Here I am a guest in your Bed and Breakfast, and you have been such a friend to me. I'll never be able to repay you for all you've done."

"Emily, this has been such a strange situation for you. I'm

glad I can help. I know I'd want someone to help me if I were in a situation like this."

Emily and Maggie entered a big room with long tables set up. There seemed to be about forty people milling around. There was a table set up for the food as well as one for desserts. Mr. Greenbush came over to where they were standing.

"Ladies, there is a table reserved for you right over here." He led them to a table where Jack and Jennifer were already seated. "If you're ready, I'll have the ladies bring out the food and then Father Jim will say grace."

"That would be fine," Emily remarked as she sat down next to Maggie.

While the food was being brought out, the people started to sit down at the various tables. Emily recognized most of them from the wake the night before. She saw Lee talking to the other men who were pallbearers. When he noticed her looking at him, he gave her a wave. She waved and turned to talk to Maggie.

"Good afternoon, ladies and gentlemen. If you'll remain seated, I'll say grace, and then we can eat this wonderful food that has been prepared by the Ladies Guild. They wanted me to say thank you to everyone who brought a dessert and salad. Now please bow your heads:

> ***Heavenly Father, this has been an unfortunate situation for Miss Jansen. Give her the strength she needs to continue on, as Liz would want her to do. Let us pray together; Bless us oh Lord and these Thy gifts that we are about to receive from Thy bounty through Christ our Lord. Amen***

Everyone murmured, "Amen."

"Miss Jansen, if you would be so kind as to start along with the people at your table, we will all follow." Father Jim stood at the head of the food table waiting for Emily.

"Please, Father, you should dish up also." Emily indicated that Father Jim should lead the way.

"Very well." Father picked up a plate and proceeded to help himself to the food.

Emily picked up a plate and surveyed the table. She couldn't believe all the food. There were meatballs, cold cuts, scalloped potatoes, potato salad, chips, green beans, cole slaw and numerous other items. She didn't have room for everything. As she went back to the table, she passed the desserts.

"I'll have to come back for dessert; I don't know which to choose because they all look delicious," Emily remarked to Maggie.

"I agree."

A lady brought around iced tea and coffee for them to drink. The people were through the line in no time. All that could be heard was a steady murmur as everyone ate.

Father Jim broke the silence, "St. Luke's parish is going to miss Liz. She was very active in the different parish ministries. It is very hard for everyone to accept that she committed suicide."

It was very hard for Emily not to tell him the truth. After taking a drink of her tea, she remarked, "I just don't believe she would have done this. She enjoyed life too much."

"I guess you just never know what might cause someone to do something like this." Father Jim shook his head.

"I guess so." Emily didn't say any more for fear of slipping up.

"Miss Jansen, what are your plans now that the funeral is over?" Father Jim asked Emily.

"I haven't given it much thought," Emily remarked putting her fork down and wiping her mouth with her napkin. "So much has happened in just a few days."

"I'm sure it all seems overwhelming. God will give you the strength you need," Father said patting her hand.

"I hope so. There are so many decisions that need to be made, and I hope I make the right ones."

"Let God be your guide, and you'll be just fine."

"Thank you, Father."

"Now you better go get some dessert before it's all gone."

"I don't think I have to worry about that. The table was filled to overflowing."

Father Jim motioned with his head toward the table, "You better take a look."

"I guess I had better get something before it's all gone."

"I'll be going now. If you need anything, please don't hesitate to call."

"Thank you. I will." Emily watched as Father Jim stopped to talk to a few people before leaving.

"I don't know about you two, but I'm getting some dessert." Emily remarked pushing her chair back and getting up from the table.

"We're right behind you," Maggie and Jack said.

"I took mine right away, so you guys go ahead, although I might just have another piece in a little while," Jennifer said as they got up from the table.

"I'm taking that piece of peach pie," Emily said taking the last piece on the table. "I love peach pie, and I don't get it very often." Maggie and Jack each took a piece of chocolate cake and followed Emily back to the table.

Jennifer was no longer at the table. "Maybe she finally left. She really just needs to mind her own business," Maggie remarked.

"Thank you, Jack, for keeping her occupied so that she didn't ask me all sorts of questions."

"No problem. I'm just glad I could help."

"Shh, here she comes," Maggie, whispered.

Emily held back a groan and pasted on a smile as she approached." Why, Jennifer, we thought you had left."

"I was talking to that nice Lee Masters. You know he is very concerned about you. He told me to tell you that if you need anything, to just let him know. He'll help any way he can."

I just bet he would Emily thought, but before she could say anything, people began coming over to her to tell her good-bye. There were all sorts of offers to help. She politely thanked everyone. Lee was the last person to talk to her.

"I'm really sorry about Liz's suicide and all. I'd be happy to help you in any way I can."

"Yes, Jennifer relayed your message. Thank you. I'll let you know if I need anything." Emily forced herself not to cringe when he shook her hand.

"Well, I must be going also," Jennifer, commented. "I'll talk to you, Emily, the next time you go to Liz's. Bye." She hurried off to try and catch up with Lee.

"That's just great. All I need is for her to come over and try to help every time I'm at Liz's house."

"Maybe she'll get occupied with something else now that this is all over." Maggie looked sympathetic. She hoped Jennifer would find something else to occupy her time and leave Emily alone.

"I better go thank the ladies in the kitchen for the meal. They did such a wonderful job."

"We'll come with you, and then we can go back to the Willow Tree and relax," Jack said, picking up his empty cup and throwing it in the trash.

"Sounds like a plan," Emily said, throwing her plate away.

The trio headed for the kitchen. "Ladies, I would just like to thank you for an excellent meal. I appreciate all the hard work you put into it." Emily said good-bye and went back out into the main room. Maggie and Jack each told the women" thanks" and joined Emily.

"Let's get back to the Willow Tree so we can all relax," Maggie suggested as they got into Jack's car. "I'm ready to get out of these clothes and get into something more comfortable."

"I'm just ready to be away from people for awhile. Most are well meaning, but you get to the point where you want to be left alone." Emily leaned her elbow on the car door and rested her head against her hand. She was beginning to get a slight headache from all the stress of the last few days.

"People knew and liked Liz. I believe she was very active in her church. She made a lot of friends in the few years she lived here. I worked with her on several occasions raising money for some charity or another." Maggie remarked.

"I knew she had worked on different fund raising projects. She seemed the happiest when she was helping someone." Emily said rubbing her forehead.

"Here we are," Jack remarked as he pulled into the driveway at Willow Tree.

"Why don't we all get changed and meet in the living room. I'll make us some iced tea and we can sit and relax." Maggie unlocked the door of the Inn, and they all went to their rooms to change.

Emily put her purse on the chair next to the door. Sitting on the bed, she fell back on the bedspread with a sigh of relief. The funeral was over, and she didn't have to be on display as she pretended that Liz was dead, stressing over every little word she said, hoping not to make a slip.

She didn't want to think about what was ahead. Trying to prove Lee was a murderer was not going to be easy. "But enough of that," Emily remarked out loud as she got up off the bed. "I will deal with that after talking with Liz tonight."

Looking through the closet, Emily took out a pair of navy Capri pants and a navy and white tee shirt. After changing her earrings and necklace, she slipped on her flip-flops and decided to open the window to let in the fresh summer air before going back downstairs.

Jack was already in the living room reading the newspaper. Maggie was bustling around in the kitchen making their tea. Emily again sat in the Queen Anne chair, but this time pulled out the footrest to put her feet on. Leaning back in the chair, she closed her eyes breathing a deep sigh. It felt like a ton of weight had been lifted from her shoulders since the funeral was over.

"Here we are," Maggie said, carrying a tray with three glasses of iced tea and a plate of cookies.

"Thank you," Emily remarked taking a glass of tea and a delicious looking oatmeal raisin cookie.

"Thanks." Jack also took a cookie to munch on. "Can't resist."

Maggie put the tray on the coffee table and sat on the opposite end of the couch from Jack. No one spoke as they sipped their tea. It was nice to just have peace and quiet.

Jack was the first to break the silence. "What do you plan on doing next? Will you be the one to take care of all of Liz's affairs?"

"I haven't given that much thought. I suppose I will have to take care of things here before I go since she doesn't have any family."

"I'm sure Jennifer Brack and Lee Masters would be happy to help you. They both expressed their desire to be of assistance." Maggie took a sip of tea, trying not to grin.

"I'm sure Jennifer would just love to stick her nose in Liz's affairs. As for Lee, I don't intend on asking him for anything."

"I get the feeling that you aren't very fond of Lee," Jack commented setting down his glass. "Do you know him?"

"I only met him once a couple of years ago when I was here. Liz knew him and didn't like him very much. He seems rather arrogant if you ask me."

"Your room will be available for however long you need it. Things are a little slow right now anyway."

"Thanks, tomorrow I'll try putting a list together of what needs to be done, and that should give me an idea of how long I will be in Hampton."

"As for me, I'm going to have another cookie," Jack stated picking one up and taking a bite.

Putting down her glass, Maggie commented, "I have an idea. Why don't we have a picnic supper? I know a deserted place out in the country where we can go and no one will bother us."

"That sounds like a wonderful idea," Emily said glad to get away.

"I like that idea," Jack said with a grin. "I get to spend time in a deserted spot with two lovely ladies, what man could resist."

Laughing, Emily and Maggie just shook their heads. "Do we know what we're getting ourselves into?" Emily asked Maggie.

"I don't know, but I think between the two of us we can handle Mr. Baker. Let me see, it's about four o'clock now. Just give me about an hour, and I will have everything ready to go. It'll take about thirty minutes to get there, and that still gives us plenty of time to eat and enjoy the scenery before it gets dark." Maggie got up and went into the kitchen to get started.

Following her into the kitchen, Emily asked, "Do you need any help?"

"No, you just relax."

"Actually I think I might go over and check on Liz's house before we go."

"I'll go with you if you don't mind. That way I can run interference if Jennifer Brack decides to come calling," Jack remarked coming up behind Emily. "We can take my car.

"Thanks, I'd appreciate that. Let me get my purse, and I'll be ready to go." Emily went upstairs and grabbed her purse from the bed.

"We'll see you in a little while, Maggie," Emily called as they went out the door.

"Jennifer is going to recognize your car from this morning and come over for sure so that she can talk to you," Emily remarked as Jack pulled into the driveway at Liz's place.

"I'll talk to her if she comes over," Jack remarked getting out of the car.

They managed to make it inside before Jennifer could spot them. Emily placed her purse on the table next to the door. "If you don't mind checking things down here, I'll go upstairs and make sure everything is okay."

Emily went upstairs all the way to the third floor first. She wanted to check the turret room and the hidden drawer with the pictures. After making sure everything was in order, she went down to the second floor and checked things there. Taking a deep breath, she quickly opened the door to Liz's bedroom, peeked in, and quickly closed it and went back downstairs. Jack was waiting for her when she came down the steps.

"Everything is fine down here," Jack said as Emily reached the last step.

The knock on the door stopped them both. They froze just looking at each other knowing that it was probably Jennifer. Jack went to open the door and was surprised to find a man standing there. "May I help you?" Jack asked trying to hide his surprise.

"I came to see Liz Marshall, but I understand that she's dead. I saw the car in the drive and thought maybe someone was here that I could talk to. The person I talked to said that Liz's friend Emily was taking care of things. Is she here, and can I talk to her?"

Jack turned to look at Emily. This must be Julia's brother Michael. She really didn't want to deal with any of this tonight. Might as well get the preliminary introductions over with, and then she could deal with this tomorrow. "I'm Emily."

"My name is Michael Crawford, and I received this letter from Liz last week. I was wondering if you knew anything about it." He handed the letter to Emily.

Emily read it over so she could talk to Liz about it. There was something she didn't like about him, but she couldn't put her finger on it. "I'm sorry, but I don't know anything about any information." Handing the letter back to him, she turned to get her purse.

"Could we just sit down and talk about this?"

"Now is not a good time. Maybe we could talk in a couple of days."

"I don't know how long I'll be in town. Now would be the best time."

"Look, Michael, Emily just buried her best friend today. She doesn't feel like talking about this now. In fact she doesn't know anything about this so-called information. Why don't you give her a break and come back some other time?" Jack stood between Emily and Michael and didn't move until Michael showed signs that he was leaving.

"Okay, I'll come back some other time. Sorry about Liz." He turned and left.

"Let's get out of here before we have a visit from Jennifer," Emily said grabbing her purse. She locked the door, and they were out of the driveway before she gave a sigh of relief.

"Do you have any idea what Michael was talking about? Had Liz mentioned any of this to you before she died?"

Emily wanted to tell Jack everything, but she didn't know if she could trust him. She would have to play it by ear for now until she was sure. There was something about Michael she didn't trust, and she would tell that to Liz tonight. "No, Liz never mentioned anything about any kind of information." Emily hated herself for not telling Jack the truth, but technically she wasn't lying. Liz hadn't told her about the information before Monday.

Chapter Six

With Jack's car loaded they headed out to the country. Maggie and Jack visited in the front seat while Emily enjoyed the scenery. Her thoughts kept going back to Michael Crawford, Julia's brother. She wasn't sure how she was going to handle this situation. At this point, she didn't know if she wanted to tell him about the evidence or not. She would discuss it with Liz when they talked later.

Before long Maggie instructed Jack to turn into a private drive. "This is where I grew up." Maggie smiled seeing the old place. "If you follow this road on back past the house and garage, it will lead you to a pond that is about a half mile from here. There is a picnic table under the trees so we can eat there."

"This is a wonderful place, Maggie." Emily was amazed at how well everything was kept up. "Do you have family around here that takes care of the place?"

"Yes, my brother and his wife live about two miles from

here. They check on things and keep the grass mowed."

"It looks like we're here," Jack said bringing the car to a stop. "Where would you like me to park?"

"You can park over by the tree where the picnic table is located. That way we won't have to carry things so far."

Emily got out of the car and stood gazing at her surroundings. The water was just as blue as it could be. Everything was so green and fresh looking. There were trees at the far end of the pond with a dock extending into the water. The hills were a deep green which accentuated the deep blue, cloudless sky.

Jack and Maggie were busy unloading the car. Emily pitched in, and soon the table was full of delicious food. Maggie had packed a picnic lunch with enough food to feed ten people. She also brought lawn chairs, so they could sit and enjoy the evening in more comfort than just the picnic table.

"Maggie, who did you think you were feeding? You have enough food for an army." Emily couldn't believe what she saw: fried chicken, potato salad, baked beans, relishes, and salad, two different kinds of dessert and tea or lemonade to drink. She also brought rolls and butter.

"She knew how hungry I was," Jack said picking up a drumstick.

"Can't you wait until we have everything ready?" Maggie scolded.

Jack just shrugged his shoulders and kept on eating.

With all the food set out, they all helped themselves to the feast. "I don't have room for everything on my plate," Emily commented. "I'll just have to have seconds so that I can try everything."

"You are a wonderful cook, Maggie. Everything is delicious." Jack helped himself to another piece of chicken.

"I second that."

"Thank you both. Just remember to leave room for dessert."

"I may have to wait till later to eat dessert. I'm beginning to fill up. I'll have to run around the pond a couple of times to get rid of everything I ate tonight." Emily pushed her plate away. "I am full, and I can't eat another bite."

"Same goes for me, Maggie. I think I'll wait till later to try your dessert."

"I'll put the food back in the ice chests, and we can save the dessert."

Emily and Jack helped Maggie clear the table. She had brought a trash bag with her for clean up. With that taken care of, they took the lawn chairs and sat a few feet from the pond.

It was a beautiful evening. There was a slight breeze that made things very comfortable. One could hear the birds in the trees and the rustle of the leaves. The atmosphere was very relaxing. Before long several ducks landed on the pond to feed. It was poetry in motion watching them glide along the water. Soon Emily spotted a deer on the far side of the pond. Without saying a word she bumped Maggie and pointed. Maggie in turn did the same to Jack. They sat without talking watching the deer drink from the pond. Before long the deer lifted its head like it was listening to the sounds around it. He turned and began walking away from the pond and out of their view.

"That was magnificent. I just love the beauty of the country. I hope some day I can find a place like this to enjoy."

"I love coming out here. I try to do that several times a month. It helps me keep my sanity."

"How about if we eat our dessert and then head back to town. It'll be getting dark soon," Jack suggested getting out of his chair.

Maggie had brought chocolate cake and cherry cobbler. "Which would you like, Emily?"

"I'm going to be a pig and have a small piece of each." Maggie put a piece of each on a plate and handed it to Emily. "Thank you."

"What about you Jack?"

"I think I'll have both also." Maggie put a piece of each on a plate and handed it to Jack. "Thank you."

Maggie decided to have the same. Before joining Emily and Jack, she put everything away so that they wouldn't have to do that later when it was time to go.

They sat in silence enjoying the food and the beautiful evening. Before long they could hear the frogs croaking around the pond. Several times a frog jumped out of the pond and sat on the bank. The sun was slowly going behind the hills, which made the sky an array of pink, purple, yellow, and blue. No one was in a hurry to get up even though it was time to head back to town.

Jack finally got up and picked up his chair. "I would prefer to sit here and enjoy this beautiful evening, but I think it is time we head back."

Maggie and Emily just nodded in agreement and picked up their chairs and put them in the car. No one talked on the ride back to town.

When they pulled up to the Willow Tree there was a car parked in front, and a man was sitting on the swing on the porch. He was in the shadows, and they couldn't see who it was.

"What is he doing here?" Emily asked when he got up off the swing and walked down the steps.

"I thought I told him you didn't want to talk to him," Jack said turning off the car.

"Who is this gentleman?" Maggie asked wondering what was going on.

Jack got out of the car ready to confront him. Emily filled Maggie in. "His name is Michael Crawford. He is Julia Masters brother. Supposedly he got a letter from Liz saying she had some information about Julia's disappearance. He stopped by Liz's today while Jack and I were over there. I told him I didn't know anything and didn't want to talk to him. At least not today."

"We better get up there before Jack does something he might regret." Maggie hurried to where Jack and Michael were talking.

"Look, I just want a room for a couple of days. I've come a long way and was told there might be something available here," Michael said trying to keep calm.

"There's another bed and breakfast in town. Why don't you try there?" Jack said through clenched teeth.

"They told me they didn't have any room for tonight."

"I do have a room, but only for two nights," Maggie remarked. "Why don't we go inside and fill out the paperwork, Mr....?"

"Michael Crawford."

"Okay, Mr. Crawford, let's get you registered."

Michael followed Maggie inside. Jack pulled Emily aside. "How do you feel about him staying here?" he asked.

"I don't like it, but at least if you or Maggie are around, maybe he won't bug me about that information and just go back to where he came from."

"It might not be a bad idea having him here. That way we can keep an eye on him. Something about this just doesn't feel right to me. I'm just not sure what it is." They went inside and sat in the living room.

"I don't want him to know which room I'm in, so I'm going to wait until he is in his room before I go up."

"Good idea. We don't need him pestering you."

Maggie led Michael up to his room, which was located on the third floor. "I do want to tell you that the front door is locked at midnight. If you go out and aren't back before then, you will be locked out." Michael nodded his head. "I serve breakfast until ten o'clock. The rest of your meals are on your own. Have a good night's sleep, Mr. Crawford."

"Goodnight." Michael went into his room.

Maggie came into the living room and sat down. "There's something about him, I'm just not sure what it is."

"I don't like him either," Emily said shaking her head.

"I hope he doesn't stay in town too long," Jack said as he got up to look out the window.

"I'm going to bed. Thank you guys for all your help today. Maggie, the picnic was just what I needed." Emily went upstairs to wait for Liz to show up.

"What information did he say Liz had?" Maggie asked quietly.

Jack turned from the window and stood with his hands behind his back. "He said that Liz wrote him a letter stating that she had some information about Julia's disappearance. The letter indicated that she might have been murdered."

"Lee said that she ran off with someone. No one ever questioned his story."

"According to Liz's letter, that might not be true."

Emily felt a gentle breeze coming in the open window as soon as she stepped into her room. The moon was beginning to rise on the horizon sending a ray of light into the room. Without turning on the light, she walked over to the window and pushed back the curtain. There was no movement of any kind outside.

"Oh, Liz, how are we going to prove that Lee killed his wife and Tonya," Emily said softly.

"We'll find a way. We have to." Liz stepped out of the bathroom where she had been hiding.

Emily jumped at her words managing to put her hand over her mouth to contain her scream. "Liz, you scared me half to death."

"I'm sorry. I didn't mean to."

"Let me turn on the light so we can talk." Emily went to the side of the bed and turned on the lamp. "I didn't expect you until around midnight."

"I sneaked up here right after it got dark. There was no one around, so I thought I would be safe."

"Michael showed up today asking about the information you had about Julia. He was here at the Willow Tree when we came back. He's staying in a room on the third floor." Emily sat on the bed chewing on her thumb.

"That's great. Maybe he can help us prove that Lee killed Julia and Tonya."

"No," Emily replied shaking her head.

"Why not? He's Julia's brother. Surely he'd want to know what happened to his sister and who killed her?" Liz sat on the bed next to Emily looking at her quizzically.

"I don't know what it is about him, but I just don't trust him. I'm getting a very bad feeling about him."

"You're instincts have always been very good when it comes to people, so I'll follow your lead on this one."

"Good." Emily gave Liz a hug. She was so grateful that she hadn't been the one killed. "Now we have to figure out a place for you to hide so that we can meet on a regular basis and not cause anyone to get suspicious."

"I've been thinking about going back to the house and hiding in one of the rooms on the third floor."

"That would be great. I can come and go from your house, and no one would suspect anything."

"Okay, it sounds like a plan. That way I can also shower and brush my teeth."

"You definitely need a shower. You're beginning to smell a little ripe," Emily said laughing.

"Thanks a lot," Liz said, giving Emily a shove. They both started laughing and then quickly put a hand over their mouths to keep from getting too loud.

"We better keep it down before we wake someone. We don't need to wake Jack; he'd be asking me all kinds of questions."

"Who's Jack?"

"He's a guest here. Actually he's a regular. I guess he comes to town every couple of months on business. He always stays here. He's pretty friendly with Maggie. He's been a big help through all this. So has Maggie."

"I'm glad you had someone to help you through all this." Liz gave Emily a hug. "Do you think Jack would be someone we could trust with this information?"

"I don't want to say anything right now. I'm not sure about anyone at the moment. We'll give it a couple of days and see what happens."

"I'll let you take the lead on this. I know we can't trust the police at the moment because Lee has them in his back pocket. They do whatever he tells them to do."

"It would be wonderful if we could trust Jack. He has been great with your nosey neighbor Jennifer Brack."

"Isn't she a pain?"

"She had the nerve to walk with us behind the casket when we went into church. She also sat with us at the cemetery. I'm surprised she didn't try to ride with us also." Emily got up and began pacing around the room.

"She is something else. I try to avoid her as much as possible. Sometimes it isn't possible, but I try anyway."

"Maggie said people cross the street when they see her coming just to avoid her."

"That's the truth. I'm just lucky enough to be her neighbor."

Emily turned suddenly and said, "You know there was a strange lady at the cemetery. She was standing all by herself and had a big black floppy hat on and was wearing sunglasses. Would you have any idea who she might be?"

"As a matter of fact I do," Liz remarked, getting up off the bed and moving toward the window.

"Who was she?"

"That was me. I couldn't resist attending my own funeral. Not everyone can say that."

"Weren't you worried that someone might recognize you?"

"I stayed far enough away, so no one could get a good look at me, and I left before all the cars left. By the way, where were you guys headed when you left the cemetery? You headed out of town."

"Jack took the long way around to the luncheon. It helped me relax a little before I had to face everyone again."

"Jack seems like a pretty decent sort of fellow."

"He is. He's been very helpful the last few days. That's why I really hope he is someone we can trust with this information."

"I better go before someone hears us." Liz gave Emily a hug and then went out the window and down the trellis.

Emily closed the window and went to bed. They had to find someone they could trust with this information. Was it Jack?

Michael quietly opened the door to his room. Checking the hallway and listening, he decided that everyone was asleep. Stepping out of his room, he closed the door without making a sound. He slowly made his way to the stairs. Staying as close to the wall as possible, he started down. When he got to the second floor landing, he listened for any kind of movement. He proceeded on down the stairs and to the front door. Turning the dead bolt and unlocking the door, he quietly opened the door and stepped out onto the porch. Soundlessly he closed the door behind him and proceeded across the porch and to his car.

Jack came out of the kitchen just in time to see the front door close. Curious as to who went out, he pulled the curtains to the side on the front door. He saw Michael get into his car and drive away. Shrugging his shoulders, Jack locked the deadbolt and went back up to his room. Whatever Michael was doing, he wouldn't be able to come back in through the front door.

Liz made it down the trellis and tiptoed to the corner of the house. Hearing a car door, she peered around the corner to see who it was. It had to be Michael's car because that was the only one she didn't recognize. Where was he going this time of night? After he pulled away, Liz ran to the cover of the trees by the street to see which direction he was heading. She got there just in time to see him turn left at the next corner. Where in the world would he be going?

After running across the street, Liz stayed in the shadows as she made her way to the corner. Unfortunately she was unable to see which direction the car went.

Lee broke the glass in the window of the back door. "We have to make it look like a burglary. We'll take a few things to make it look that way."

He stuck his hand through the broken window and opened the door. Turning on his flashlight, he proceeded through the kitchen.

"Where should we start?" Michael shined his flashlight into the living room.

"Why don't we start upstairs? We'll start on the third floor and work our way down. If we leave the place a mess the police will just think it was kids breaking into a dead person's house and stealing a few things."

They went up the stairs to the third floor. There were just three rooms. Two of the rooms were completely empty and the other one just had a chair in it. They moved to the second floor. Most of the rooms had unpacked boxes in them.

"Should we check all of the boxes? That would take forever," Michael commented as he shined his flashlight around the room.

"No, if we don't find what we're looking for, we'll do that another time. Let's go to Liz's bedroom and check through things there."

In Liz's room, Michael began going through the dresser, and Lee started looking though things in the closet. They were both just making a shambles of the room.

Lee went through the boxes stacked on the shelf. He just threw things on the floor as he went through each box. He pulled out a suitcase that was on the floor of the closet and opened it up. It was full of clothes. He pulled everything out looking for the pictures. There were several purses in the closet also. Lee took them out one at a time and went through them throwing the items from the purses onto the floor.

One purse had an old driver's license of Liz's and a couple of credit cards in the wallet. He grabbed the cards and threw the rest on the floor. There was one last purse on the floor. Picking it up, Lee went through its contents. He pulled out the wallet and looked at the driver's license. The name on it was Tonya Murphy, not Liz Marshall.

"Hey, Michael, look at this," Lee called. "I wonder if Liz had an alias. There's a driver's license and credit cards in the name of Tonya Murphy." Lee picked up the license he had just thrown on the floor to compare them.

"They sure look like the same person," Michael commented, looking over Lee's shoulder. "Maybe she did have an alias."

"The one that says Tonya Murphy is an Illinois license." Lee put both licenses in his pocket. "We'll have to check into that further. Did you find anything?"

"No, I sure didn't."

"Where could she have hidden those pictures?" Lee looked around the room. Going over to the bed, he lifted up the mattress to see if they might be there. "Damn, where could they be?"

"Let's go back downstairs and check things out there," Michael suggested, going out of the bedroom.

"Might as well."

They went through all the drawers in every room making a

shambles of the place. Lee came across Liz's dark room. Her camera was on the counter along with various negatives that she had hanging up. None of them were the pictures he was looking for.

"Do you think she put them in a safe deposit box?" Michael asked.

"My contact at the bank never said anything. I'll check with her tomorrow and find out for sure. Let's get out of here. Grab the television and VCR.

Michael took the television, and Lee grabbed the VCR, and they went out the same way they came in. They took off through the backyard to where their cars were parked a couple of blocks away.

"Tomorrow you can come out to see me, and we can discuss our next step." Both Lee and Michael took off.

Liz got to her garage and sat in the shadows enjoying the night air. She really didn't want to go up to the stuffy attic just yet. She noticed a light moving around on the second floor of her house, and then it disappeared. Shaking her head, she figured her imagination was playing tricks on her. Slipping through the side door of the garage, she decided she really didn't want to be outside not knowing for sure whether she was imagining things or not. Just as she closed the door, she heard voices coming from the house. She went to the window next to the door and saw two men coming out of the house carrying something. She couldn't make out what they were carrying. As they came out of the shadow of the house, she could see them pretty clearly with the full moon. The one person definitely was Lee Masters, but she couldn't make out whom the other person was. It looked like the other person was carrying her television. She couldn't make out any more as they reached the shadows of the trees. Going back to the door, Liz locked it before going up the steps to the attic above the garage.

Michael went back to the Willow Tree. When he tried to get in the front door, he found that someone had locked the door and the dead bolt. Taking a small case out of his pocket, he easily unlocked the dead bolt and then opened the lock on the door. Quietly he let himself inside and locked the door as well as the dead bolt. After listening for any movement in the house, he went up the stairs stopping on the second floor landing and listened making sure all was quiet. When he was assured that all was well, he continued up the stairs to the third floor. He unlocked his door and went inside. Without turning on the light, he undressed and crawled into bed.

Jack opened the door to his room and listened. He could have sworn he heard someone moving about. Satisfied that all was quiet, he went back to bed. Lying there, Jack wondered exactly what the information was that Liz had that showed Julia might have been murdered. He also felt that Emily knew more than she was saying.

Chapter Seven

Emily was up and dressed early. She wanted to have all day to get things figured out so that Liz could stay at her house without anyone knowing. Hurrying down the steps, she stopped short when she got to the dining room and saw Michael sitting at the table eating breakfast. She really didn't want to talk to him, but felt she had no other option except to have breakfast and hope he didn't ask her a lot of questions.

"Good morning," Michael said when Emily walked into the room. "Hope you had a pleasant sleep."

"I slept very well, thank you." Emily didn't like his overly chipper attitude. She busied herself by filling her plate with the food that was on the sideboard. Maggie had again outdone herself. With her plate full, Emily poured herself a glass of juice and then sat down at the table. Deciding she also wanted some hot tea, she got up and poured a cup of tea.

"Good morning," Jack said cheerfully. "It looks like Maggie made another great breakfast." He proceeded to dish up his plate and then sat at the table next to Emily. "I hope you slept well Emily."

"I did, Jack."

"Michael, I hope you had a pleasant night's sleep."

"I had a great night's sleep."

"You slept all night long without interruption?" Jack asked quizzically.

"You could say that."

"Good morning, everyone. I hope you all had a wonderful night's sleep. I know I did."

"I had a good night's sleep." All three said in unison laughing.

"I didn't think my question was funny," Maggie remarked, checking the food on the sideboard.

"That has been our entire conversation since we came down to breakfast," Jack told Maggie.

"No wonder everyone laughed at my question." Maggie picked up the empty dishes and went back to the kitchen.

"Now that we got the question of everyone's sleep out of the way, what are your plans for the day, Emily?" Jack asked taking a sip of his coffee.

"There are a few things that I have to take care of, but nothing pressing. It will be a quieter day then the last few have been." Emily took a sip of tea and continued eating.

"Is there anything that I can help you with?" Jack asked, finishing his cup of coffee. He rose to help himself to another.

"It is really too bad about Liz," Michael said as he finished his breakfast.

"Yes, it is," Emily, remarked quietly.

The ringing of the phone interrupted their conversation. The three of them could hear Maggie talking to someone.

"You have a phone call, Emily," Maggie said coming out of the kitchen. "There's a phone by the staircase that you can use."

"Thanks, Maggie." Emily wiped her mouth and placed her napkin next to her plate. She went out to the entryway to take her phone call.

"This is Emily...Yes, I see...I was planning on going over to the house shortly...You'll meet me in an hour...That's fine, see you then." Emily hung up the phone and went back to the dining room. After finishing her breakfast, she went into the kitchen to talk to Maggie.

"Did you get your phone call all right?" Maggie asked when she saw Emily.

"Yes, thank you. I just wanted you to know that I will be over at Liz's house if someone should want to get in touch with me. I'll see you around noon."

"See you later." Maggie looked at Emily as she walked out of the room. She wondered whom the phone call was from.

Emily went back into the dining room. "See you all later." Emily continued through the room and went upstairs. Picking up her purse, she checked herself in the mirror. With a shrug, she turned and left, closing and locking the door behind her. Hurrying down the steps, she went out to her car.

Jack went into the kitchen to talk to Maggie. "Did Emily give you any idea where she was going?"

"My, aren't we nosey."

"I just want to make sure she'll be all right."

"If you must know, she was going to Liz's."

"Maybe I'll drop by there later. I wonder who her phone call was from?"

"I don't know, and I didn't ask because it's none of my business." Maggie busied herself washing the dishes.

Before getting out of the car at Liz's place, Emily looked around to make sure that Jennifer Brack was nowhere in sight. Not seeing anyone, she got out of her car and went up to the house. After letting herself in, Emily laid her purse on the table next to the door. It took a moment for her eyes to adjust to the dimness. Emily walked into the living room stumbling over something. She made her way to the window and opened the curtains. Turning around, she surveyed the room in horror. The place was a total disaster area. The books from the bookcase were everywhere. The drawers were open, and the contents thrown about the room. The television was gone from the stand.

Emily went into the dining room and found a similar scene. Drawers open with the contents thrown all over the room. All the rooms downstairs were the same. The window on the back door was broken, and that was obviously how the intruder or intruders came in. Not wanting to disturb anything, Emily got her cell phone out of her purse to phone the police.

While she waited for the police, Emily went upstairs to check things out. Liz's bedroom was completely torn apart. The dresser drawers were open with things thrown about. The closet was open, and all the boxes on the shelf were thrown on the floor along with their contents. Purses, clothes, everything was thrown about the room. They had even thrown over the mattress.

Emily quickly went up to the third floor to check the turret room. She was relieved that the pictures where still in the hidden drawer. Closing the drawer, she hurried back down stairs to wait for the police. Just as she reached the bottom step she heard the sirens. "Oh, great. That definitely will bring Jennifer Brack running." Emily shook her head and went to open the door.

Detective Daniels was coming up the walk when she opened the door. "So, what's the problem this time? A simple little break in?"

"I'm sorry to have disturbed you Detective," Emily said sarcastically. "But it's more than just a simple little break in. Whoever did this trashed Liz's house." Emily stepped aside so that the Detective and his men could enter.

Detective Daniels sent two men into the kitchen while he walked around the living room. "You didn't touch anything, did you?" He said slipping on rubber gloves. "You could compromise the crime scene if you did."

"No, Detective Daniels, I didn't touch anything. I called you from my cell phone."

"Do you know if anything was taken?" Daniels looked around the living room writing down notes every so often.

"The television was taken, and I believe also the VCR. I really couldn't say if anything else was." Emily just wished they would hurry up and finish their business so that she could start cleaning up.

"Hey, boss," One of the officers called from the kitchen. "I think we found out how they got in."

Detective Daniels followed by Emily went into the kitchen. Broken glass was all over the floor in front of the back door.

"It appears that the perpetrator broke the glass on the door and then reached his hand inside and unlocked the door."

"That's what it looks like. Dust the door for fingerprints, but I doubt if we find anything." Daniels continued looking around the kitchen and making notes. "When you're done, come upstairs. I'm going to start checking things out."

Emily followed Detective Daniels up to the second floor landing. "Nothing was disturbed on the third floor."

"I think we should take a look anyway," He remarked heading up to the third floor.

He went into the rooms and looked around. They were empty, so there really wasn't anything to see. When he came to the turret room, he walked around stopping just a foot away from the hidden drawer. Emily held her breath as she waited for him to move on.

"Looks like everything is fine here. Let's go back down to the second floor."

They went down to the second floor, and Daniels opened each door and looked around as he made his way down the hallway. Liz's bedroom was at the end of the hall.

"This is Liz's bedroom," Emily said as he opened the door.

Stepping inside, Detective Daniels surveyed the mess. "They really had fun in here." He walked around the room taking more notes and not saying anything more.

Soon the two other officers joined them in the bedroom. One started taking pictures while the other one carefully dusted for fingerprints. Emily just stood back watching them work. The ringing of the doorbell sent her rushing down the stairs.

"Please, don't let it be Jennifer," she said quietly. Opening the door, she was surprised to see a gentleman standing there. "May I help you?"

"I'm Pete Jones. We had an appointment, but it looks like you might be a little busy," he commented looking at the police cars.

"As a matter of fact, I am. Someone broke into the house last night, and the police are here investigating."

"I don't want to bother you at this time, so why don't I leave this with you, and we can get together tomorrow." Pete Jones handed Emily a large manila envelope. "It contains a copy of Liz's will and some other papers that she had me draw up."

"I will look this over tonight and call you tomorrow morning to set up a time to meet."

"That'll be fine. I'll wait for your call." He turned and went to his car.

Detective Daniels and his men were coming down the stairs as Emily closed the front door. "I think we're finished here."

"Do you have any clues as to who might have done this?"

"To tell you the truth Miss Jansen, in my opinion, I think it was kids who read about the death of your friend in the paper and decided they would see what they could find to sell and make some money."

"How can you be so sure?"

"It happens all too often."

"That doesn't say much for the young people in this town if they make a habit of doing something like this."

"Not all young people, just a couple of bad apples. You have them everywhere."

"So you're not going to investigate any further? You're just going to assume that it was kids?"

"I didn't say that," Detective Daniels remarked, getting defensive. "We will continue to check all the evidence and see if we can solve this case. Oh, by the way, if you should notice any of Miss Marshall's credit cards are missing, let me know."

"I'm not sure what cards she had, but if I discover any mailings or anything from credit card companies, I will let you know."

Emily watched them walk to their cars. Before going inside, she saw Jennifer hurrying across the street waving her arms and shouting something. Emily wanted to run inside and lock the door, but knew she couldn't stop the inevitable. May as well just get it over with.

"Oh, Emily, what happened?" Jennifer said breathlessly.

"Someone broke into Liz's house last night. You didn't happen to notice anything unusual, did you?"

"I didn't, but then when I fall asleep, I'm out."

"Thank you for stopping by, but I really need to get back inside and clean things up."

"I'd be happy to help you with that." Jennifer was excited at the prospect of snooping through all of Liz's things.

"That's quite all right," Emily said, taking Jennifer by the arm and leading her down the porch steps. "I can mange just fine on my own. Thank you for the offer. I'll talk to you later." Emily left Jennifer standing at the end of the sidewalk and turned, hurrying back into the house. The last thing she needed was for Jennifer to help her clean up.

Where to begin, Emily thought as she looked around. The first thing was to get the window on the back door fixed. Picking up her cell phone, Emily dialed the Willow Tree.

"Thank you for calling the Willow Tree Inn. This is Maggie. How may I help you?"

"Maggie, hi, this is Emily?"

"Hi, Emily. What can I do for you?"

"I need the name of someone who can fix a broken window."

"Oh my, did you break a window on your car?"

"No, someone broke into Liz's house last night. They broke the window on the back door to gain entrance. The police just left."

"Emily, that's terrible. Is there anything I can do?"

"Thank you, no."

"If you do, let me know. Now, I always use Joe's Repair. They fix just about anything. I believe he can replace the window."

"Thanks a lot, Maggie. I'll see you later."

Emily found the number in the phone book. She talked to his receptionist. Joe was out on a call, but she would give him the message so he could call her back.

After cleaning up the glass from the broken window, Emily went into the living room to survey the mess. Might as well just start right in; putting off picking things up wouldn't make it go away. The doorbell stopped her in her tracks. Whoever was there could just go away, she didn't want to deal with anyone right now. The bell rang again. With a deep sigh, Emily went to the door. Upon opening it, she was relieved to see that it was Jack.

"Thank goodness it's you. I was afraid that Jennifer had come back."

"Maggie told me about the break-in, so I came by to see if you could use some help."

Before she could say any more, her cell phone rang. "Hello...Yes, this is Emily Jansen...You'll be by around two o'clock...Great, I'll see you then...Bye." With a sigh of relief, Emily put her cell phone in her pocket. "The repairman will be here about two o'clock to fix the window on the back door."

"Did the police have any ideas about the break-in?" Jack asked looking around.

"Detective Daniels thought it might be kids."

"Why kids?"

"He figured they probably saw Liz's obituary in the paper and knew the house would be empty."

"Really. Did they take anything?"

"About all I can tell is the television set, and I'm assuming she had a VCR, but I can't be certain of that. I really don't know what else might have been taken."

"Do you mind if I look around? Maybe I can notice something the police might have missed."

"No, go ahead." Emily proceeded to pick up the books and put them back on the bookshelves.

Jack went into the kitchen to check out the back door. He noticed that there was a piece of glass sticking up and looked at it more closely. It looked like there was something on it, so he found a towel to use to pry it loose. Holding it up to the light, he examined it further. A box with plastic bags was lying on the counter, after pulling one out; he dropped the glass into the bag and put it in his pocket.

"Did the police dust for prints from the back door?" Jack

asked coming into the living room.

"They did, and they also took pictures of the back door. Why?"

"I was just wondering. Do you know if there was any blood in the area of the door or on the door?"

"That I don't know. If they did find anything, they didn't say anything to me." Emily finished putting the last book on the bookshelves, and she then began straightening the cushions on the furniture. It was beginning to look a little better.

"Do you mind if I look around upstairs?"

"No, I don't mind. You don't have to go up to the third floor though. There isn't anything in any of the rooms." Emily didn't want him alone in the turret room with the possibility of his finding the hidden drawer.

There were rooms up and down the length of the hallway on the second floor. Jack opened each door and checked inside. Most of the rooms just had boxes in them that hadn't been disturbed. One had several boxes along with a mattress and box springs leaning up against the wall. The last room at the end of the hallway was in complete disarray. This obviously had been Liz's bedroom. Stepping inside, Jack just shook his head.

"They really made a mess of things, didn't they?" Emily said as she entered the room.

Jack turned to her and shook his head in agreement. "It makes you wonder what they were looking for."

"I haven't had a chance to clean up this mess. I wanted to get everything done downstairs first." Emily picked up the alarm clock and the box of tissues.

"You know," Emily remarked with a sigh. "Detective Daniels wouldn't even listen to me when I told him that Liz never took pills, especially sleeping pills."

"Why are you so sure that Liz didn't take sleeping pills?" Jack asked, taking a chair from the corner of the room and bringing it to Emily so that she could sit down.

"For one thing, she had trouble swallowing pills, and for another her father killed himself by taking a bottle of sleeping pills when she was ten years old. She was the one who found him. She was terrified of taking sleeping pills. I told this to Detective Daniels, but he wouldn't listen."

"Why wouldn't he listen to you? That is some very important information that would shed a different light on the situation."

"It was because Lee Masters brought in a letter supposedly written by Liz saying that she killed his wife Julia Masters."

"Did you see this letter?"

"Yes, he showed it to me. It was done on a computer, and the address was typed, so anyone could have written it. Supposedly it was Liz's signature, but that could have easily been forged. He wouldn't listen at all." Emily sat there shaking her head trying to hold back the tears.

Squatting down next to Emily, Jack took a tissue and handed it to her. "Detective Daniels seems to be a little short sighted, not checking into all the information. Seems in a bit of a hurry to close the case on Liz's death."

"And on this break-in, blaming it on kids." Standing up, Emily took a deep breath. "I'm really sorry to bore you with all this Jack. I wasn't planning on saying anything, but I couldn't keep it bottled up any longer."

"You didn't bore me. I found it quite interesting. I'm getting hungry. Why don't we go have lunch and come back to this later? I think you need a break."

"Why not? I'm afraid this mess won't go away."

"Why don't you just ride with me," Jack commented as they went downstairs.

"Fine, I'll meet you at your car. I just need to check on the garage and make sure everything is okay in there. It'll just take me a minute."

"I'll wait for you in the car."

While Jack went out to his car, Emily headed for the kitchen and went out the back door. Unlocking the garage door, she went inside. There was no glass in the big garage door so; Jack wouldn't be able to see anything.

"Liz," Emily called quietly.

"Hi, Emily. What in the world has been going on? I noticed the police were here."

"I can't get into it right now. Jack is waiting to take me to lunch. We'll talk later. How are you?"

"I'm fine."

"I have to go, but I thought that maybe you could sneak inside the house after dark tonight."

"That would be great, and then we can find a place for me to hide."

"I'll talk to you when I'm by myself later. It won't be unusual for me to go into your garage, so no one should suspect anything."

"Great, I'll talk to you later."

"Bye." Emily gave Liz a quick hug and went back outside. She made sure to lock the door behind her. Coming back into the kitchen, Emily locked the back door laughing as she did so. "A lot of good that will do."

She picked up her purse and went out to the car by Jack. "Let's get some lunch."

At the café, Emily and Jack went inside. They found an empty booth and sat down. The waitress brought over menus and took their drink order.

"Everything sounds good," Jack commented looking over the menu. "Have you decided what you're going to have?"

"I'm not sure, I don't want a hamburger, but I'm not sure what I want. The hot ham and cheese on toasted French bread sounds good though."

"I think I'm going to have a nice juicy hamburger and fries." Jack closed the menu and laid it to the side.

"Can I take your order?" the waitress asked taking out a notepad and pen.

"I'll have the half pound hamburger and fries," Jack told the waitress.

"What would you like?" asked the waitress turning toward Emily.

"I'll have the hot ham and cheese on toasted French bread."

"Would you like barbeque sauce with that?"

"Yes, please."

"Would you like French fries or homemade potato chips?"

"I think I'll try the homemade potato chips. Thank you," Emily said, handing her menu to the waitress. Leaning back against the seat, she remarked, "This certainly wasn't what I had planned for my stay with Liz."

"Things don't seem to be getting any better for you either. Now having to deal with this break-in." Jack picked up his glass and took a sip and put it down. "So our illustrious detective thinks it was kids who broke in."

"That's what they're leaning toward. I don't think they are going to check any further."

"It sounds like Daniels likes to close cases quickly without really having all the facts." Jack picked up his napkin and placed it in his lap.

The waitress brought their meal, which basically put an end to that line of conversation. After filling their drinks, she waited on some other customers.

"So, how's your sandwich?"

"It's great. I like the barbeque sauce with it, and the chips are really good," Emily remarked, taking another bite. They both concentrated on their food, leaving no room for further conversation.

Back at the house, they both went into the kitchen to start cleaning up. The doorbell rang right at two o'clock. It was the repairman. He came into the kitchen and measured the window and said he would be back shortly to put in the new glass. Less than fifteen minutes later he returned with the new glass and quickly had everything done.

"That looks great," Emily said after he had finished. "If you can figure the bill, I can pay you right away."

"I'll just go out to my truck and write the ticket for you." After figuring everything, the repairman came back in with the bill and handed it to Emily.

She wrote out the check and gave it to him. "Thank you very much for your prompt service."

"You're welcome. Here's my card if you need anything further. You have a nice day now." With that he was out the door.

"Things are looking pretty good down here," Jack stated putting the last item in the cupboard.

"Yes, they are. I really do thank you for all your help today."

"No problem, I'm just glad I could do it. Do you want me to help you upstairs?"

"No, thank you. I think I can manage that myself. Actually, I've decided to move in here while I'm in town."

"Do you really think that's wise?" Jack asked a little concerned by Emily's decision. "What if whoever broke in comes back?"

"I don't think that will happen if someone is here all the time. Besides, there are a lot of things that need to be taken care of, and it will be easier for me if I am staying here."

"I can't talk you out of doing this?"

"No, you can't. I think I'll go back to the Willow Tree and pack my things so that I can get moved this afternoon."

"If you need anything, just let me know." Jack didn't like the idea of Emily staying there, but he knew there was no talking her out of it. Best to go along with things, so he could help if she needed it.

"Thank you, Maggie for all your help." Emily gave her a hug before she went out the door. "I'll call you if I need anything. Thanks, Jack, for all your help."

"I'm here if you need anything, and I'm sure I'll be stopping by from time to time."

"I'd like that. Bye." Emily went out to her car and took off.

"Things sure have quieted down around here in a hurry," Maggie remarked, closing the door.

"Well, you still have a couple of guys to keep you on your toes," Jack joked, picking up the newspaper from the table.

"Actually, Michael checked out about an hour ago." Maggie headed into the kitchen.

"Oh, he did? Was he going back to California?" Jack followed Maggie into the kitchen and sat down on a stool by the island in the middle of the room.

"He kind of hinted that he was, but he really didn't say one way or another when I asked him directly."

Chapter Eight

Moving away from the window Liz looked at her watch. It was only four o'clock. Opening the trunk that was next to her, Liz looked through its contents. She was glad to have something to occupy her time. If she didn't, she would have gone crazy. The last few days had been very hard on her, having to pretend that she was dead. Until Lee was arrested she had no choice but to continue to play dead. At least she would be hiding in her own home where she could take a shower and wash her hair. It had been almost a week since she was able to do that, and she could barely stand herself.

The trunk was full of old newspapers. She took one out and held it close to the window so she could read it. It was dated 1942. The previous owners of the house had left a couple of trunks and several boxes of stuff in the attic of the garage. They hadn't wanted any of the items and told Liz she could keep them. There were items in every dark corner also. The last few days had given her time to begin looking through everything to see if there was anything of value. Not having any light made it a little difficult to do a lot of searching.

Digging a little deeper into the trunk, Liz found an old book covered in dust. Paging through it, she found that it was a history of the house and the area around Hampton. This she would take with her inside and read at another time when she had plenty of light. When everything had settled down, she would come up here and have a good look at the old stuff that was left. It could prove mighty interesting.

Emily opened her car trunk and took out her suitcases along with a basket from Maggie. She was glad about her decision to stay at Liz's. This way she and Liz could work on figuring out what to do, and no one would get suspicious. Unlocking the house, she set her bags in the entry and closed and locked the door behind her. She wanted to talk to Liz briefly before she went to get a few groceries. With her staying there, she didn't need any kind of excuse to go out to the garage. No one would wonder why.

Maggie had sent a care package with her so she wanted to give Liz something to eat to hold her over until supper. Putting the basket on the kitchen cabinet, Emily took out a piece of chicken and a piece of chocolate cake. This should hold Liz until later. There were bottles of water on a shelf in the garage, so she didn't have to worry about taking anything to drink.

As Emily came down the back porch steps, she realized that the side door to the garage could be seen from the street. It might look funny if she took a plate of food to the garage and didn't come out with it. Seeing the garbage can she knew what she could do. Turning around she went back inside and covered the plate in aluminum foil. She then put the plate carefully inside the garbage can and carried it to the garage.

Inside she set the can down and took out the plate of food. Carrying it to the stairs she quietly called out, "Liz, its Emily." When she didn't get a response, she called out a little louder, "Liz, it's Emily."

"Hi, Emily," Liz said, coming down the stairs.

"I brought you some food to hold you over until you come in tonight. I'm going to make supper, so you can eat later."

"That sounds wonderful." Liz took the plate and took off the foil. "This looks delicious."

"Maggie gave me a care package when I left the Willow Tree. I brought my things and intend on staying here with you."

"I'm glad." Liz began eating the chicken and had it down in nothing flat. "I'm sorry, I'm making a pig of myself."

"That's okay. I have to tell you that someone broke into your house last night and trashed the place."

"I saw two people in the back yard last night. It looked like one of them was carrying something. It almost looked like my television set."

"They did take it. I need to get back inside, and we can talk about the break-in once you come inside. See you later." Emily gave Liz a hug and then went back to the house.

Once inside Emily decided to leave her bags by the stairs and make a list of groceries that was needed. She managed to find a pen and paper going through Liz's kitchen. Several things in the refrigerator would need to be thrown out, but Emily figured she could do that later. Right now she just wanted to see about a few basics and take a look at what meat Liz had in her freezer.

With the list made, she grabbed her purse and went out the door to her car. Emily was just about to get into her car when Jennifer came charging across the street hollering for her to wait. She pasted a smile on her face and tried not to look annoyed.

"I'm so glad I caught you. I saw you were carrying suitcases before. Does that mean you plan on staying in the house?"

"Yes, I'm going to stay here."

"I hope you know what you're doing. What if those hooligans come back?"

"Detective Daniels seems to think the reason they broke in was because no one was living here. If someone is staying here, then they shouldn't come back and bother things. If you'll excuse me, I have some grocery shopping to do."

"Great, so do I. I'll go get my purse. I'll just be a second." Jennifer hurried back across the street to her house.

Emily could have kicked herself for saying what she was going to do. Now she would have to put up with Ms. Nosy.

"I'm ready to go," Jennifer said getting into the car. "Won't this be fun now that we're neighbors?"

"Oh, yeah, fun, like a toothache," Emily thought. The downtown area was quiet without a lot of traffic. Emily parked her car and just suggested meeting back there in a half hour. She didn't want to have Jennifer following her around when she was trying to shop.

"Okay," Jennifer agreed. "I'll meet you in half an hour."

After going grocery shopping, Emily went back to her car. She was surprised to see Jennifer waiting for her. "I hope you haven't been waiting long." Emily said putting her packages in the trunk.

"No, I just got back here a few minutes ago. Did you get everything done that you wanted to do?"

"Yes, I did. Did you?"

"Yes, everything taken care of."

When they arrived back at the house, Jennifer thanked Emily for taking her along and left, much to her amazement. Taking the sacks out of the trunk, she went into the house to put them away. She was going to make spaghetti with meat sauce and garlic bread. That wouldn't take long, so she didn't have to start it yet since she was going to wait to eat when Liz came in.

"So did you say anything to Maggie as to what your plans

were?" Lee sat at his desk, putting his hands behind his head and leaned back in his chair.

"She asked me if I was leaving town and I just hinted that I might be. If she assumes that I did, then that is her mistake now isn't it." Michael sat in the brown leather chair in front of Lee's desk. "So what's next?"

Lee straightened up picking up the driver's license that was lying on his desk. "I think that Tonya Murphy happened to be in the wrong place at the wrong time." Throwing the license on the desk, Lee got up and went to the window. "That means that Liz is out there somewhere, and we have to find her. She may have the pictures with her since we couldn't find them in the house."

"There were some places that we didn't look. We could always go back there and check things further."

"That would be too risky right now. I think I need to pay a little visit to Emily very soon. I'm sure Liz has gotten in touch with her by now. If they were such good friends, she surely wouldn't let Emily continue to think she's dead. I have a feeling Emily knows where Liz is hiding. We just have to find a way to get it out of her. You'll have to hang around here for a while. Some people might wonder what's going on if they see you around town."

"I can hang around here." Michael made a sweeping gesture with his hands putting his feet up on Lee's desk. "It's a lot better than what I've got in California. In fact, I think I could get used to this."

"Just don't get too used to it because it's not permanent," Lee walked around his desk and gave Michael's feet a shove knocking them off his desk.

Jack dropped the envelope into the slot at the post office. Walking back to his car, he just couldn't get rid of the gnawing feeling he had that something wasn't right about Michael's leaving town. Why would he come all this way and then just leave without talking to Emily again if he was so interested in finding out the truth about his sister? It just didn't make sense. Picking up the paper that was on the seat beside him, he thumbed through the pages looking for the classified ads. Taking a pen from his pocket, he circled two ads. Putting his car in gear he took off down the street.

Emily gazed around the bedroom looking at the mess. She wanted to at least start cleaning up before Liz got there, but she knew she would need her assistance in putting things away. Pulling on the mattress, she was able to remake the bed. Chills ran down her spine when she smoothed the pillow and bedspread where Tonya had been lying. Wrapping her arms around herself, she tried to control the shaking that overcame her. Hurrying to the door, Emily turned out the light and closed the door. Maybe when Liz was with her, they could take care of things.

Downstairs Emily went out on the porch to enjoy the warmth of the summer day. She didn't know about Liz, but she knew that she wouldn't be able to sleep in that bed. They would have to make other arrangements, like sleeping on the mattress in one of the spare rooms.

Feeling better after being in the fresh air, Emily decided to go ahead and make supper. She was making spaghetti, so it would be something easy to warm up later. The garlic bread could be made while they warmed the spaghetti. The activity of making supper lifted her spirits, and she began to feel better about the idea of their staying in the house.

Hearing the doorbell, Emily wiped her hands on the towel and turned the burner off under the sauce. She figured it was probably Jack checking up on her. "Hi," she said cheerfully as she opened the front door, stopping short of saying anything further when she realized it wasn't Jack.

"Hello." Seeing the look on her face, Lee remarked, "I gather that cheerful 'hi' was not for me."

"You're right. It wasn't. I thought you were someone else.

What do you want?" Emily stepped outside on the porch and closed the door behind her.

"I came with an offer." Lee walked over and leaned against the porch railing crossing his arms in front of him.

"I really am not interested in any offer you might have." Emily leaned against the house and crossed her arms in front of her.

"Now, that's not very neighborly of you. You could at least hear me out."

Emily could see that Lee was trying to remain civil, but she could see his eyes begin to narrow. "You're not my neighbor, so I don't feel I have to be neighborly, but I will listen to your offer." She didn't want to provoke him too much at the moment. "So, what is it?"

Lee stood up and moved closer to Emily. "I would like to buy this house." He stood just a foot away from her towering over her.

Emily said a silent prayer and relied on everything she had inside her to stand up straight and look him in the eye. She wasn't going to let him know how much he really frightened her. "I'm sorry, Lee, but the house is not for sale."

"What do you want with this thing? You don't even live here." Lee clenched his fists trying not to make a scene. No one tells him "no".

"I don't have any say about selling this house."

"Didn't Liz leave you this house? I know her lawyer was here to see you."

Emily was surprised and angry by what he just said. "So you have been spying on me? Are you keeping track of who comes to see me? You have a lot of nerve!" She restrained herself from slapping his face.

"Look, you're not from here, but everyone knows that I do as I please in this town, and no one crosses me." Lee took a step closer to Emily.

"Well, hello, Lee. Hi, Emily. Am I interrupting something?"

Emily was surprised to see Jennifer standing next to her. She was never so glad to see anyone in her life, even if it was Jennifer. "Hi, Jennifer. No, you weren't interrupting. Lee was just leaving."

Lee turned and stormed down the steps to his pickup. He tore off down the street leaving tire marks in his wake.

"Are you okay, Emily?" Jennifer asked touching her arm. "Lee looked very angry."

"He was. I'm so glad you showed up when you did. I don't know what he might have done." Emily leaned back against the house breathing a sigh of relief.

"You must have made him very angry."

"Lee doesn't like someone to tell him 'no'."

"Why don't we sit on the swing for a moment." Emily allowed herself to be led to the swing by Jennifer. "You don't have to talk. Just try and forget this whole thing.

Emily was surprised that Jennifer didn't try to pry any information out of her. She just sat quietly next to her. Taking a deep breath, Emily finally began to feel better. "Thank you for coming by, but I need to get back in the house." She got up and walked to the door.

"I'll talk to you later," Jennifer said heading down the steps.

Once inside Emily closed the door and locked it behind her. She couldn't believe that Lee was watching her. He must be getting very desperate. They had to find someone to help them and quickly.

With the cover of darkness, Liz slowly opened the door of the garage and peeked out. The back yard was dark enough that she shouldn't be seen running up to the house. The street light in front of the house was out again for which she was glad. Tucking the book under her arm, she ran across the yard. She quickly went up the steps of the back porch and turned the knob on the door. As quietly as she could, she slipped inside. The kitchen was dark and empty. The aroma of spaghetti filled her nose and caused her stomach to growl. Liz hadn't realized just how hungry she was. Laying the book on the cabinet by the door, she reached for the light switch jumping when the light came on before she had a chance to turn it on.

Emily muffled a scream when she saw someone standing in the kitchen. "Thank goodness it's you, Liz." She put her hand on her chest in a sigh of relief.

"I'm sorry, Emily, I didn't mean to startle you." Grabbing her hand, Liz gave it a squeeze. "I'm starving, but I think I'm going to take a shower and wash my hair before I eat anything."

"While you're doing that, I'll warm up the spaghetti and make the garlic bread. I haven't eaten anything because I wanted to wait and eat with you." Emily turned on the broiler so she could put the garlic bread in the oven.

"I'll go up and take a shower. I'll try not to be too long." Liz headed out of the kitchen to go upstairs.

"Liz, wait. I'll go with you." Emily turned off the oven, so she could go upstairs and prepare Liz for what she was about to see.

They ascended the stairs in silence. As they walked down the hall, Emily broke the silence. "I haven't cleaned anything up in your room Liz. I just want you to realize that it is going to be a mess."

Liz slowly opened the door to her bedroom. She had tried to prepare herself for what she might see, but she wasn't prepared for this. It took her a moment to fully grasp everything. Turning to Emily, she said, "I think I'll just get a few things and take my shower in the other bathroom. I don't think I can be in here right now."

"I figured as much so I put the mattress and box spring down in the other room and got it ready for us to sleep on tonight."

"Thank you. I'll just get my stuff, and then you can go downstairs, and I'll take my shower." Liz forced herself not to look at the bed and went into the bathroom to get her toiletries. She also picked up a package of underwear that they hadn't torn open. She was grateful that they hadn't. Everything would have to be washed before she could wear any of it. Stopping in front of the closet, she just shook her head, letting the tears fall that she had been holding back.

"If you want to borrow some of my clothes for tonight, you can," Emily said quietly, putting her arm around Liz. "I'll get you something to wear while you get in the shower."

Liz nodded gratefully. Brushing away the tears she went down the hall to the other bathroom. Emily opened her suitcase and pulled out a pair of lightweight sweat pants and a matching t-shirt. Picking up the bra she bought before she left home, she decided to have Liz wear it. They were the same size, so it made things very convenient.

Knocking on the bathroom door, Emily called, "Liz, I'm coming in, and I have some clothes for you when you're done with your shower. I also have a new bra here for you to put on."

Peeking out from behind the shower curtain, Liz smiled. "Thanks, I really appreciate everything."

"I'm going downstairs to fix the garlic bread and warm up the spaghetti."

"Okay," Liz called out after her. She stood in the shower letting the hot water pour over her. Seeing her bedroom in shambles and her bed where Tonya died just took everything out of her. The tears flowed down along with the water. With the tears gone, Liz picked up the shampoo bottle and lathered her hair. It felt so good to finally get to wash her hair. Lathering the sponge, she scrubbed herself trying to feel clean. The soap cleaned her body, but she still felt so violated with everything that had happened.

Back downstairs Emily turned on the broiler and the burner under the spaghetti. Taking the garlic bread out of the freezer, she put it on a cookie sheet and put it in the oven. Grabbing a stool from the corner of the kitchen, she put it down next to the cabinet. She sat down placing her elbow on the counter and resting her head in her hand. She had set the table earlier, so she just had to finish the meal.

She picked up the potholder that was hanging on the wall by the stove and opened the oven checking on the bread. It was almost done, and she had to watch it carefully, so it wouldn't burn. Taking the spoon from the spoon rest, she took the lid off the kettle and stirred the spaghetti. It was beginning to steam, so she knew it was almost ready. Opening the oven, she checked the bread again. Turning it off, she took the bread out and set it on the butcher-block table next to the stove. Removing the kettle from the burner, she turned off the stove.

Liz stood in front of the mirror and combed her hair. It felt fantastic to be clean. The scent of the food below made its way to the bathroom. Her stomach growled again causing her to hurry and finish getting dressed. She felt like a new woman now that she was clean and took the stairs two at a time.

"Have a seat in the dining room," Emily said when she saw Liz in the doorway. "I'll dish up the plates."

"Better put plenty on mine. I'm starving," Liz said laughing.

"There are plenty for seconds if you need more," Emily called, as she dished up the food. She set the plate of spaghetti and garlic bread in front of Liz and then sat down herself.

Liz sprinkled parmesan cheese over her spaghetti and then took her first bite. "Mmmm. This is so good." She took another bite before putting down her fork and taking a bite of garlic bread.

Emily just smiled as she watched her. She couldn't imagine going almost a week without eating much of anything. She dug into the food in front of her enjoying Liz's reaction.

"I think I had better slow down," Liz said wiping her mouth on her napkin. "It's been awhile since I have had a meal to eat that I might have a bad reaction if I gobble my food."

"Take all the time you need. I'm in no hurry."

They ate in silence for a while just concentrating on the food. Emily was so glad that Liz was with her so that now they would be able to put their heads together and get things figured out. They needed help and had to find someone they could trust. She was leaning toward Jack, but she wanted to run it past Liz before she said anything to him.

"Do the police have any idea who might have broken in?"

"They think it might have been kids knowing that the place was empty."

"Do you think it was just kids?" Liz asked, picking up her glass.

"Actually, I think it was Lee looking for the pictures,"

"That wouldn't surprise me at all."

"By the way, Liz," Emily remarked putting her fork down. "Your attorney was here today and gave me some papers to look at. We have an appointment tomorrow."

"That would be my will along with some other legal papers. Have you read any of them?" Liz asked wiping her mouth. She picked up her glass and took a drink of water.

"No, I haven't taken the time to read them. I really don't want to keep the appointment with Mr. Jones tomorrow."

"You have to," Liz remarked firmly. "If you don't, someone may become suspicious."

"You're right. I know I have to." Emily took a sip of her water and set the glass down. "I will be so glad when we can stop pretending that you're dead."

"You and me both."

"To the phoenix rising and Lee going down," Emily said, picking up her glass.

"Here, here." Liz picked up her glass and touched Emily's.

With the dishes all done, Emily and Liz went into the living room. There was no television to watch since it had been stolen. They sat on the couch enveloped in the quiet. It was very relaxing after everything that happened.

Emily got up from the couch and went into the entryway and picked up the envelope from Mr. Jones. Taking it back into the living room, she sat on the couch next to Liz.

"I guess now is as good a time as any to look at these. Unless you want to tell me what they say?" Emily remarked looking at Liz.

"No, I'd rather you read them," Liz commented shaking her head.

Emily couldn't control the tears that welled up in her eyes as she read Liz's will. She had left everything to her including the house. Reading through the pages, she just shook her head in disbelief.

Liz moved over next to Emily and gave her a hug. Pretty soon they both were crying. "Don't we make a pair?" Liz said laughing.

"We sure do. I guess that's why we've been friends all these years." Emily placed the papers on the coffee table. "Liz, does anyone else know what is in your will?"

"Only my attorney. Why do you ask?"

"Lee stopped by earlier and wanted me to sell him your house. There wouldn't be any way that he would know anything about your will is there?"

"Not that I know of. Maybe he was just assuming you would be the one to inherit everything since I didn't have any family."

"Maybe you're right. He has been watching the house or someone is watching the house for him because he knew that your attorney was here today."

"I'm sure he has spies everywhere. I was thankful that the streetlight was out when I came into the house tonight. I was afraid someone might have been watching."

"It is dark enough in the backyard, so I'm sure no one saw you come in." Emily hoped her words were true and no one had seen Liz.

The clock in the dining room stuck midnight. The sound in the silence seemed to echo throughout the house.

"I think it's time for these two Cinderellas to go to bed before we turn into a couple of pumpkins," Emily said with a chuckle, getting up from the couch.

"That sounds like a good idea. I'm ready to sleep on a mattress and lay my head on a pillow." Liz got up and followed Emily upstairs.

Opening the door to one of the spare rooms, Emily turned on the light. She had found a set of sheets along with two pillows and a light blanket. The bed looked very inviting.

"I do have an extra pair of pajamas for you." Emily picked them up off the bed and handed them to Liz. After turning on the light on a small table next to the bed, Emily turned out the top light.

Liz quickly changed her clothes and put on the pajamas. Crawling into bed, she sighed. "This feels wonderful. It was absolutely horrible sleeping in that dirty attic. This is heaven."

"I can't imagine what you have been through. It must have been terrible."

"The thing that kept me going was knowing you were here, and some how we were going to make sure Lee went to jail for what he did to Tonya and Julia."

"I'm going to open the window, so we can let some fresh air in." Emily got out of bed and went to the window. There was a gentle breeze coming into the room after she opened it. "This should help you sleep," she said turning around. Liz already was sound asleep. Smiling, Emily stood for a moment just watching her. She was so glad that she hadn't lost Liz. Getting back into bed, she turned out the light. "Pleasant dreams, Liz," she whispered. Turning on her side, she hoped to sleep.

Chapter Nine

The smell of bacon frying tickled Emily's nose. Grinning, she slowly woke up. "Ah, Maggie is making one of her great breakfasts," Emily said stretching and opening her eyes.

Realizing very quickly that she wasn't at the Willow Tree, she sat up in bed. She had slept better than she figured. It was good to have Liz with her. Getting out of bed, she grabbed her robe and went downstairs.

"I hope you're hungry," Liz remarked as Emily entered the kitchen. Taking the last piece of bacon out of the frying pan, she placed it on the platter. Turning off the burner under the hash browns, she placed them on the platter with the bacon and put it in the oven to keep warm.

"I'm starved as usual. Can I help with anything?"

"You can make some toast. I'll scramble up some eggs for us."

"Where do you keep the toaster?" Emily asked opening up a cupboard.

"It's in the cabinet next to the back door." Liz broke several eggs and whipped them with a wire whip before pouring them into the pan.

"Found it," Emily said, taking the toaster out of the cabinet and setting it on the counter. "Hey, what's this?" She picked up the book that was on the counter and took it over by Liz.

"Oh, that. I found it in one of the trunks that are in the attic above the garage. It's about the history of this house and Hampton."

"This looks interesting," Emily said thumbing through the pages. "I'll put it on the dining room table for now."

"Yeah, put it down and get back to work making the toast."

"Okay, you don't have to get bossy," Emily, joked. It was great to be able to laugh with Liz. They always had a good time together.

With the toast and eggs done, Liz took the platter of bacon and hash browns out of the oven and along with the eggs put everything on the dining room table. Emily brought the toast, and the two of them sat down to enjoy their breakfast.

"How did you sleep last night, Liz?" Emily asked before taking a bite of her eggs.

"I slept like a baby. When I woke up, I felt energized." Liz spread jelly on her toast before taking a bite.

"I slept well also. I wasn't sure how I would do last night when we went to bed, but it didn't take long for me to fall asleep." Emily put her fork down, wiping her mouth and hands on her napkin. "You know Liz, we need to figure out a place for you to hide when someone comes by or when I'm gone just in case someone tries to break in again."

"You're right. I guess I could hide in one of the closets upstairs."

"That might work. Whenever I leave we'll have to make sure it looks like only one person is living here so we need to make sure your clothes and toiletries are all put away."

"Could we wash some of my clothes so that I have something to wear? That wouldn't look suspicious, would it?" Liz didn't want to put any of her clothes on without washing them first. Not after a stranger had touched them. She shuddered thinking about it.

"That shouldn't be a problem. I can always say that I'm washing them so they're clean when I take them to Goodwill." Emily wiped her hands on her napkin and pulled the book Liz had found closer to her so she could page through it.

"I'm glad. I don't think I can wear them before they're washed." Liz took a drink of her orange juice. "I didn't have much of a chance to look at the book while I was up in the attic. I didn't have much light to read by." She took the last bite of her hash browns and put her fork down.

Emily continued to finish eating and paging through the book. "Look what it says here." Picking up the book, she put it on the table between the two of them. "It says this house has a secret room."

"Let me see that," Liz said, wiping her hands on her napkin and leaning over to read what it said. "I wonder if it's in the room where we're sleeping?"

"I don't know. It kind of sounds that way. You know, that would be the solution to our problem of where you can hide."

"Why don't we go and check it out," Liz remarked, getting up from the table.

Emily got up to follow her upstairs, but stopped at the bottom of the steps. "I think we should clean everything up first in case someone would come by. They might wonder why two people were eating breakfast when I'm supposed to be here by myself."

Liz stopped at the landing and turned around. "You're right. That might look a little suspicious."

Together they made light work of the clean up. Emily thought they should just wash up the dishes and not leave them in the dishwasher. They didn't need anybody snooping and seeing all the dishes. With the kitchen and dining room back in order they took the book and headed upstairs.

Lee stopped his truck in front of the Willow Tree. "I think a little visit with Maggie today is just what I need." Getting out of his truck, Lee strutted up the sidewalk like a peacock fanning its tail feathers in front of a peahen. Stepping inside, Lee looked around in admiration at what Maggie had done to the old house. With a little bit of money, though, she could really spruce the place up he thought.

"Hi, may I help you," Maggie said, walking into the entryway. She stopped short when she saw it was Lee.

"You've done very well for yourself," Lee said waving his arm around the room.

"Thank you. So, to what do I owe this visit?" Maggie walked behind the desk in the corner of the entryway.

"Why, I just wanted to see how you were doing." Lee walked over and stood in front of Maggie. "How has business been?" He leaned over trying to see what she had on her computer screen.

Maggie closed the window saying, "Business has been just fine, but I'm really surprised that you would be interested."

"Oh, Maggie, I'm interested in everything you do." Lee took his cowboy hat off and ran his fingers through his hair and then put it back on.

"Like I said, business is just fine, so you can leave now." Maggie was trying to figure out exactly why Lee was there. In the five years that she had owned the Willow Tree, he hadn't set foot in the place.

"Maggie, Maggie, Maggie, I'm a businessman, and you're a businesswoman. I think we could do some business together that would profit both of us immensely.

"I really don't think so," Maggie remarked shaking her head.

"Come on, Maggie. What are you afraid of? Having money?" Lee walked around the desk to where Maggie was standing and put his arm around her shoulder.

Maggie cringed at his touch. Taking his hand, she removed it from her shoulder. "I do quite well, and I'm very happy with my life. Thank you anyway." She moved around the desk and walked over to the front door.

"I can bring you a lot of business. I have people that come to town to see me, and I can recommend that they stay here. I would pay you well to take care of my guests." Lee placed his hand against the door so that she couldn't open it.

"And what would I need to give you in return for all this business you send my way?" This was not the Lee she had fallen in love with in college and almost married. He started hanging out with the upper crust at school, and he became a different person.

"Maggie, you cut me to the chase," Lee said dramatically, putting his hand on his heart. "Why do you think I would want something in return?"

"Everyone knows you don't just do something out of the kindness of your heart. There's always a catch to it."

"There really isn't anything I want you to do for me. Just maybe keep me informed of the people who come and go around here and what they might be up to. That's not so bad, is it?" Lee pushed his cowboy hat back on his head and tried to look so innocent.

"Like?" Maggie asked questioningly.

"Oh, like Jack and Emily just to use an example." Lee said shrugging his shoulders.

"It's time for you to go," Maggie remarked, opening the door.

"Be seeing you around Maggie." Lee strutted down the sidewalk to his truck.

Maggie stood watching him wondering just what he was up

to. Before getting in his truck he waved to her. She shut the door without waving back. Why was he concerned about what Jack and Emily were up to? Things just kept getting more and more strange.

"Are you sure this is the right closet?" Emily asked as she felt along the molding at the back of the closet for something to trip open the back wall.

Liz picked up the book and reread the passage. "This has to be the right one." She laid down the book and squeezed in the closet beside Emily.

Liz pounded the wall up above Emily while she pounded around on the closet wall below hoping something would happen. They weren't having much luck.

"Shh," Emily said touching Liz on the leg. "I thought I heard the doorbell."

"The front door is locked, isn't it?" Liz whispered.

"Yes, I haven't even touched it yet today," Emily, whispered in reply.

"Why are we whispering?" Liz asked as she sat on the floor next to Emily and leaned back against the wall.

"I don't know. There isn't any one around to hear us," Emily said in her normal voice.

Liz adjusted herself and leaned back against the wall. Before she knew what was happening, she was on her back looking up at a bunch of cobwebs.

"How did you do that?" Emily exclaimed in excitement.

"I don't know," Liz said standing up and dusting herself off. "I just moved my buns around a little and the next thing I know, the wall opened."

"So the trigger mechanism must be on the floor." Emily went back inside the closet to try and find it. The lighting was not good, making it difficult to see much of anything. "Do you have a flashlight?"

"There's one in the nightstand in my bedroom."

"You stay here, and I'll be right back."

Emily hurried down the hallway to Liz's bedroom. Going to the nightstand, she opened it and took the flashlight. "I've got it," she called coming back into the room.

It took some careful examination, but finally they discovered a little pin action lever that when compressed would open the door. One would definitely have to know it was there in order to trigger it. The hook on the back of the door could be used to pull it closed once the person came back into the closet.

They propped a box in front of the door so it wouldn't go closed while they looked around the secret room. Emily shone the flashlight on what appeared to be a small room furnished with an old couch and table next to it. As they walked around checking things out they found stairs leading down.

"Why don't we see where they go?" Liz said, getting more curious by the minute.

"I better stay here in case the doorbell rings. Here you take the flashlight and check it out. Just be careful." Emily handed the flashlight to Liz and watched as she went down the stairs brushing the cobwebs out of the way.

"There had better not be any big spiders down here," Liz said nervously. "Everyone in town would hear my scream."

Just then the doorbell rang. "Try to be as quiet as you can, and I'll get rid of whomever it is as fast as I can."

"I'll be as quiet as a mouse. And I hope I don't run into any either," Liz remarked going down the wooden stairs.

Emily closed the closet door and went downstairs to see who was at the door. She wiped her hands on her pants and opened the door to find Jack standing there. "Hi, Jack," she said, trying not to sound out of breath.

"Hi, is everything okay? You sound a little winded."

"I'm fine, I was just up on the third floor and hurrying down the stairs got me a little winded." Emily couldn't believe how easy it was to make something up on the spur of the moment.

"Makes sense. I can't stay, but I just wanted to give you my cell phone number in case you would need to get a hold of me at any time. I moved out of the Willow Tree."

"So does that mean you're leaving town?" Emily said, hoping not to sound too disappointed.

"No, I'm not leaving town. I moved into an apartment since it looks like my business will be keeping me here longer than I expected."

"Your business is doing well then?" Emily asked curiously, happy that he wasn't leaving town.

"You might say that. If it's not a problem, I might drop by this evening if that's okay with you."

"That will be just fine." Emily tried to control how happy she was feeling.

"I'll see you later." Jack went back to his car and took off down the street.

Emily hurried back inside making sure to lock the door. She went upstairs to see how Liz was faring with her exploring. "How are things going?" Emily called down the stairs to Liz.

"I'm at the bottom," Liz called back. "There must be another secret door just like up there."

"Be careful. I don't want you getting hurt."

"I'll be careful."

"Liz? Are you all right?" Emily called after waiting for what seemed like an eternity. "Liz? Answer me. Liz?"

"Yes." Liz remarked touching Emily on the shoulder causing her to jump.

"Where did you come from? You know you scared me half to death." Emily wanted to be angry with Liz, but was just relieved that she was all right.

"Follow me." Liz led Emily out of the room down the stairs and to the kitchen.

"Okay," Emily said giving Liz a puzzled look.

Liz opened the broom closet to reveal the hidden door at the bottom of the staircase. "This is where the stairs lead. Right here to the kitchen."

"This is great," Emily exclaimed with excitement. "This means that no matter if you're upstairs or down here, you can get to the secret room." Hugging Liz, she continued, "That book is great."

"Speaking of the book. I think we should put it in the secret room so that no one else can get that information."

"Good idea Let's go do that right now." Emily looked at the clock in the kitchen while Liz closed the secret door and the door to the broom closet.

"I better call your attorney. I told him I'd give him a call this morning and set up another appointment with him.

"I'll go up and take care of things while you do that." Liz left the kitchen and went upstairs.

Emily picked up her cell phone and dialed Mr. Jones' number. "Hello, this is Emily Jansen, and I would like to speak to Mr. Jones please....Thank you...He's busy?...I wanted to set up an appointment....Yes, I can come in at three o'clock....Okay, thank you...bye."

Emily put her phone down just as Liz came back down stairs. "I have an appointment at three o'clock this afternoon. I really wish I didn't have to do this."

"There's nothing to worry about. He'll just go over the will with you, and then that will be it. Nothing can happen anyway until it goes through probate and that usually takes several months. This will all be over, and I'll be out of hiding." Liz was trying to convince herself as much as she was trying to convince Emily.

"You're right. Now how about if we tackle the mess up in your bedroom and get some of your clothes washed."

"It definitely won't get done if we don't do it. Let's go."

"Do you have a clothes basket?" Emily asked before going upstairs.

"Yes, it's in the laundry room. I'll go get it and meet you upstairs." Liz took off toward the kitchen and opened the door to the laundry room. Picking up a basket, she hurried upstairs.

Standing in the doorway to Liz's room, they just looked at the mess and shook their heads. "Why don't you pick up your clothes and put them in the basket, and then I'll take them downstairs to wash," Emily finally said.

"I can do that," Liz said going over to her dresser and started to pick up her clothes.

Emily stood in front of the chest of drawers and straightened the figurines that had been knocked over. Bending down, she reached to pick up an angel statue that she had given to Liz. She fought back the tears when she saw that one of the wings had broken off when it hit the floor. Kneeling down, she found the wing a short distance from where she had found the statue.

Liz came up behind her continuing to pick up her clothes. "What did you find?" She knelt on the floor next to Emily.

Emily just lifted the statue and the wing to show Liz without saying a word.

"Damn, Lee," Liz said through clenched teeth.

"I'll get some glue when I go out later and try to fix it", Emily said quietly.

Liz just shook her head "yes", not wanting to say any more in case she started crying.

Emily stood up and set the statue on the chest of drawers for the time being. She offered her hand to Liz and helped her up. "I see the basket is full, so I'll take it downstairs and start the washer."

"Bring the basket back up when you come up, and I'll pick up the rest of the clothes then." Liz had at least picked up her lingerie to be washed first. She just hated the thought of them going through her intimate things.

"I'll be right back." Emily took the basket and went downstairs.

Liz went back to the dresser and started putting her jewelry away. She had one jewelry box that sat on top of the dresser and another one that contained all her mother's jewelry. That one she kept in the bottom drawer of the dresser. They had taken that one out and rifled through all the jewelry and then threw it onto the floor. She picked up the old tin box that was her mother's and tried to straighten the one side that had been bent when it hit the floor. The tears just fell. She didn't try to stop them.

Carefully picking up each piece of jewelry, she examined it and then gently put it back in the box. The last piece of jewelry was a strand of pearls that her father had given her mother when they got married. It was very old and very delicate. She could see that it was broken before she picked it up. Getting up, she looked around and found a small ceramic dish with a lid. Back on the floor she carefully picked up the pearls and placed them in the dish. With each pearl she picked up, she became angrier. She would use her anger to keep her going in making sure that Lee was brought to justice.

The doorbell rang just as Emily was about to go back upstairs. She set the basket down and opened the front door.

"Oh, did I catch you in the middle of something," Jennifer asked curiously.

"Yes, you did," Emily said not offering anything further. She really didn't want to be rude to her since she had been so helpful yesterday when Lee was there, so she added, "Is there something I can do for you, Jennifer?"

"No, I just wanted to see how things were going for you. You know that I would be happy to help you with the clean up."

"I appreciate your offer, but I can manage. Thank you anyway."

"Well then, I guess I'll be seeing you around, neighbor." Jennifer took off down the steps turning and waving when she got to the street.

Emily waved back and closed and locked the door. Picking up the basket, she went upstairs. "It's getting close to lunch time, so why don't we pick up the rest of your clothes and go back downstairs and make us some lunch," Emily said walking into the bedroom.

"I'm really not very hungry, but I think I could use a break. This is taking a lot more out of me than I figured it would. I am just so angry at Lee." Liz stood up and placed the dish on the dresser. She then put her mother's jewelry box back in the bottom drawer.

"I am too. We'll make sure he gets caught and pays for his misdeeds." Emily picked up the rest of the clothes, and they went downstairs.

After putting the basket in the laundry room, Emily checked the refrigerator to see what might be good for lunch. "Hey, Liz, there's some of Maggie's chicken left and also some fruit that she sent over. We could have that if you like?"

"That sounds good. I might just have a piece of chicken and some of that fruit." She took a couple of bottles of water from the fridge and then fixed herself a plate. It would have been nice if they could go into the backyard to eat, but she knew that wasn't a possibility. The dining room table would have to do.

Emily filled her plate and took the water, sitting down next to Liz at the table. "You know," she remarked putting the piece chicken on her plate. "We have to find someone we can trust to help us. Do you know anyone we could give this information to that we can trust?"

"I don't know of anyone. Everyone in this town either works for Lee or is afraid of him, so they won't do us any good."

"I do have someone in mind." Emily picked up her water and took a sip.

"Who might that be? Jack?" Liz guessed.

"He's the only person I feel would be willing to help us, and he isn't from here. The only other person I know is Maggie."

"I've heard she had a relationship with Lee when they were in college. In fact, I heard that they were engaged at one point, and that she called it off."

"Interesting. I wonder why she called things off." Emily finished her chicken and then ate the rest of her fruit.

"I never did hear." Liz took a long drink of water and sat the bottle on the table. "Emily, if you think Jack is the person we should tell about Lee and everything he has done, then I think we should do it and not waste any more time. I'm ready to see that Lee pays for what he has done."

"When I talked to him earlier, he said he might be by tonight. I'll call him later and make sure he is coming by."

"Sounds good." Liz picked up her paper plate and took it to the kitchen to throw away.

"Why don't we clean up the secret room? This way when you have to stay up there later, it'll be a little more comfortable." Emily finished wiping off the table and hung the dishcloth on the rack on the inside of the cabinet door.

"At least I can use a flashlight while I'm in there and won't have to worry that someone might see the light."

They made the room as comfortable as possible, first sweeping up the dirt and cleaning away the cobwebs. Using the vacuum cleaner Liz vacuumed the couch the best she could. It still wasn't the best, but it was better than it had been. Emily dusted the table next to the couch, and with that they called it good.

"I better get cleaned up so that I can keep my appointment with Mr. Jones. I hope it doesn't take long, so I can get back here and we can finish cleaning up your bedroom."

"I plan on doing a little reading while I wait for your return," Liz said holding up the book she had found in the attic. "I think this could prove quite interesting."

Emily checked herself in the mirror one more time before leaving the bathroom. She stopped to see Liz before leaving, giving her a hug and closing the secret door behind her and making sure the closet door was closed.

At Mr. Jones' office, she told the receptionist her name and then took a seat. It was only a matter of a minute or two before Mr. Jones came out, and they went into his office.

"Please have a seat, Miss Jansen," Mr. Jones said, indicating one of the chairs in front of his desk.

Emily took a seat. She always had a hard time deciding what to do with her hands when she was nervous, so she put her purse on the chair next to her and rested her hands on top of the envelope of papers.

"I assume you had time to read over the papers I gave you."

"I'm just surprised at the amount of holdings that Liz has, and that she would leave everything to me."

"Yes, Miss Marshall has done quit well for herself. Now, since you have already read everything, I think the only thing to discuss is a timeline of when the property will be legally yours." Mr. Jones leaned forward and folded his hands.

"I'm not familiar with any of this, so exactly how long does something like this take?"

"First, the will has to be probated which usually takes about three months. During this time, a notice is published in the local paper asking if there are any creditors. This is published three times. After the three months and no creditors come forward, it all becomes yours." He sat back in his chair waiting for her to speak.

"I wouldn't be able to do anything about the house before that?"

"Correct."

"You take care of all of that?"

"Yes, you don't have to do anything."

"Is there a hearing?"

"Yes."

"Do I have to be there?"

"No."

"Is there anything else, Mr. Jones?"

"That pretty much takes care of things."

"I will go then, and I thank you for taking care of things. Thank you." Emily stood up and extended her hand.

Mr. Jones shook her hand. "I'll be in touch when everything is final."

"Thank you again."

When Emily got out of Mr. Jones' office, she saw Jack across the street. He was talking on his cell phone and didn't see her. She called to him as she crossed the street. He ended his conversation and waved to her.

"Hi, what brings you downtown?" Jack asked as Emily stepped up on the curb.

"I had to meet with Liz's attorney about her will. I'm glad that's over with. I'm glad I saw you because now I won't have to call you."

"And why were you going to call me?" Jack asked raising his eyebrow.

"When I talked to you this morning, you said you might come by the house this evening."

"That's right."

"I was just checking to see if you were coming by because I need to talk to you about something very important." Emily nervously chewed on her bottom lip.

"Yes, I was planning on stopping by for a few minutes this evening."

"Good. Then I'll see you about...?"

"Probably about seven thirty."

"Great. I'll see you then." Emily stepped off the curb to go back to her car.

Jack stood looking after her wondering what she needed to talk to him about. Shrugging his shoulders, he figured he'd find out soon enough.

Emily took the stairs two at a time. She was excited that they would soon be sharing their information with someone else. It had been very hard keeping everything secret. Opening the door to the closet, she sprang the pin to open the secret door.

Liz looked up as the door opened. "You're back already?"

"I gather you weren't bored while I was gone." Emily sat on the couch next to Liz.

"This book is fantastic. There is some very interesting history to this house."

"Why don't we pick up in your bedroom, and you can tell me all about it. By the way, Jack will be here this evening, so we can tell him everything."

"Good." Liz stopped inside her bedroom trying to decide what to take care of next.

"You know," Emily remarked, picking up one of the purses on the floor. "We should probably check and see if anything is missing from your purses."

Sitting on the floor, Liz and Emily started gathering the items from the purses. It took quite awhile to sort through everything.

"It looks like all my credit cards are missing and my drivers license." Liz remarked, putting things back in her purses.

"Is this purse Tonya's?" Emily asked, holding up the bright green bag.

"Yes, it is."

"Do you see her driver's license or any credit cards in her name?"

"I know she had some because I saw them when she got here," Liz said, looking through the items left on the floor.

"If Lee did this, and he has that information, then he knows that you are alive."

Chapter Ten

"Come in Jack," Emily said, opening the door. She stood to the side to allow him to enter. "Why don't we have a seat in the living room."

"You said there was something you needed to talk to me about." Jack sat down on the couch.

"There is," Emily remarked nervously. "I'm not sure where to begin."

"How about at the beginning." Jack was growing more curious by the minute.

"I'll be right back." Emily left the room and went upstairs.

Jack looked after her wondering what was going on. He had never seen Emily so flustered even through the wake and funeral.

Emily came into the living room. "Jack, there's someone I want you to meet."

Jack rose from the couch wondering who it could be.

"This is Liz Marshall." Emily moved to the side, and Liz appeared from behind the doorway.

"Liz Marshall!" Jack said in disbelief. "I thought you were dead!"

"Why don't we all sit down, and Liz and I will explain everything." Emily sat on the opposite end of the couch from where Jack was sitting. Liz sat on the chair next to the couch.

"Okay, so explain to me why you aren't dead and who was buried this past week."

"Before we begin, you have to swear that you won't tell a soul from this town about this. Especially not Lee Masters. The reason we're telling you is because we need your help."

"I have no intention of talking to anyone in this town, especially Lee Masters." Jack leaned back on the couch trying to get more comfortable.

"I guess to give you a clear picture of what happened, I need to go back about six months or so and start from there." Liz was a little nervous talking about the chain of events to Jack, but she knew they had to trust someone, and Emily felt they could trust him so she would trust him also.

"About six months ago I was out taking pictures in the country. Lee had said I could come on his property by the woods and the stream any time to take pictures. I didn't have to let him know."

Emily put her hand on Liz's arm to stop her. "Before we go on, how about I get us some tea to drink?" Liz nodded. "Jack would you care for some?"

"Yes, thank you."

"I'll be right back."

Jack didn't know what to say to Liz while they waited for Emily to return. It was shocking that she was alive, but he was glad for Emily. He knew how much she loved Liz.

"Here we are." Emily came in carrying a tray with three glasses of tea on it. She served Jack first and then walked around the coffee table to where Liz was seated. She helped herself. Putting the tray down, Emily sat on the couch picking up her glass and taking a sip.

Liz took a sip of tea and then set her glass on the table next to her chair. "Okay, to continue. That day while I was taking pictures, I heard a plane flying very low. I saw it through the trees. It circled once, and then it sounded like it was landing. I took off on foot in the direction of the sound." Liz stopped and took another sip of her tea. She stood up and began walking around the room.

"I could see in the distance a clearing where the plane had landed. I didn't want to get too close, but I wanted to see what was going on. I used my camera with its telephoto lens and started snapping pictures."

"Was the clearing on Lee's land?" Jack asked leaning forward.

"Yes. I had heard rumors of an old airstrip around here somewhere, but I didn't know exactly where it was. This must have been the one." Liz stopped and sat on the hassock with her hands clenched together tightly.

"What did you see?" Jack asked anxiously waiting for Liz to continue.

"I saw Lee and a couple of his men go out to the plane and meet the pilot as he got out of the cockpit. They stood talking for a short time, and then Lee motioned to someone standing by a little tool shed." Fear gripped her as she recalled what she had seen. Lee was capable of anything, and she hoped they were doing the right thing by telling Jack.

"It's okay, Liz, go on." Emily got up and sat on the hassock next to Liz and put her arm around her.

"The next thing I saw was the man by the shed bring a woman who had her hands tied and tape over her mouth."

"Did you recognize this woman?"

"Not at first, but as I looked at the pictures when I enlarged them, I saw that it was Julia, Lee's wife."

"What did they do with her?"

"She was struggling to get away as the man brought her over to where Lee and the pilot were standing. Once she got there, Lee backhanded her across the face, and then they put her on the airplane. After they put her on the plane, Lee handed the pilot an envelope. The pilot then got back into the plane, and it took off. I knew this was something I shouldn't have seen. I took off and got back home as quickly as I could so that Lee wouldn't know I had been there." Liz started shaking, and Emily gave her a squeeze to comfort her.

"Who else knows about this? Jack asked amazed at what he was hearing?

Liz composed herself and continued. "I didn't say anything to anyone. When I heard that Julia had run off with someone she met on the internet, I knew it wasn't true. I kept hoping that she would come back, but she never did. I didn't know what to do or who to tell. Lee owns the police in this town and I knew they wouldn't do anything about it."

"What does this have to do with the events of this past week?"

"About two weeks ago, I decided I would just inform Julia's brother that I had some information about her disappearance and say nothing more. I'm not sure how, but Lee found out that I had some pictures that could incriminate him in regard to Julia."

"Could Michael have informed him that you had some information?" Jack definitely felt that Michael was the leak in all this.

"I didn't think so at first, but since talking to Emily, he's the only possible answer."

"So that brings us up to last week when Emily arrived to find you dead only, it wasn't you."

Liz got up and sat back down on the chair. After taking a sip of her tea, she continued. "On Sunday my cousin Tonya arrived out of the blue. We hadn't seen each other since we were kids, so I was very surprised to see her. Apparently her mother had just died and she was working out the loss by visiting her long lost relatives. The family always joked that we were twin cousins since we looked alike."

Liz tried to keep the tears in, but to no avail. They streamed down as reality sank in. Emily handed her a tissue. "That morning I went for my usual walk. Tonya was just waking up and was going to take a shower while I was gone." Taking a deep breath, she dabbed her eyes trying to compose herself.

"I was only gone about a half hour, no more. I returned from walking through the woods behind the house. Before I came out of the woods I noticed a man walking around the side of the house. He looked around the back yard, turned, and went back around the house. That's when I crept closer to have a better look. When I heard voices, I looked around the side of the house and saw a black, four door, short bed pickup drive away."

"Did the pickup have any other distinguishing features?" Jack asked taking a little notepad out of his pocket.

"Yes, it had silver racing stripes on the side."

"Do you know anyone in town that has a pickup like that? Jack asked taking notes.

"There's only one truck in town like that, and it's owned by Lee Masters."

"What happened next?"

Liz closed her eyes and saw Tonya lying on the bed. Opening her eyes, she continued, "I called out to Tonya as I went through the house to the stairs. When I didn't hear anything, I rushed upstairs to my bedroom. She was lying there. Lee had killed her, thinking she was me. I knew Emily was on her way and thought about waiting for her, but I didn't want to chance Lee returning and finding me, so I went out to the garage and hid in the attic."

"When did you find out that Liz was alive?" Jack was amazed by what this young woman had been through.

"I found out that she was alive the second night I was here. She came to my room at the Willow Tree." Emily smiled at Jack's reaction.

"How did she get to your room without being detected?" Jack remarked knowing that he didn't see anybody come and go.

"I climbed up the trellis that was outside Emily's window in the middle of the night. Her window was open just enough so that I could push it up and crawl inside."

Jack just shook his head. "That is just amazing. Where do you have the pictures?"

"I hid them in a secret drawer in the turret room on the third floor. I'll go get them." Liz took off upstairs to get the pictures.

"Your friend is a very special person to be able go on after all she has been through." Jack had difficulty comprehending the whole situation.

"Here are the pictures." Liz handed the envelope to Jack.

As he looked through the pictures, he said, "These are definitely something Lee would kill for."

"There's one more thing." Liz left the room for a moment.

Emily wondered what it was. Liz hadn't mentioned anything else.

Liz returned and handed Jack a memory card from her camera. "The pictures that are there are just a few of the pictures that I took."

"You never told me about that. Where did you have it hidden?" Emily was totally blown away.

"I really had forgotten about it until now. I hid that in a drawer with a false bottom in my dark room. I didn't want to have the pictures and the memory card together."

"Smart thinking." Jack was pleased by her calm thinking in all this. "Now I want you to put the pictures back up in the secret drawer where they were. I'm going to take this memory card. The camera I have uses the same type of card.

"Then I won't need to lend you my camera," Liz said, sitting back in the chair.

"No," Jack said, putting the memory card in his pocket.

"I always knew you were very level headed in a crisis, but I'm amazed by all this." Emily felt very good about the situation, and that Lee was going to pay for what he did.

"I know someone with the state police. I can get this evidence to them so that we can get the ball rolling and put Lee Masters behind bars for a long, long time."

"Thank you. I'm sorry I didn't say anything sooner, but I really didn't know who to trust. You were always so helpful I hated not being able to tell you everything." Emily was so glad that they had finally told him the truth.

"I understand your hesitation considering the circumstances. There is one thing I would like to know Emily."

"What is that?"

"How were you able to pretend that it was Liz in that coffin and go through with the funeral?" Jack was overwhelmed by everything they both had been through.

"I had to so that Lee wouldn't get suspicious. I didn't think I had it in me, but I guess you do what you have to do. I just kept visualizing Lee in jail."

"How are you feeling about everything, Liz?" Jack asked.

"It has been very hard. Talking to you tonight about everything that happened has made me feel so much better, that someone actually believes me." Liz felt like a weight had been lifted from her shoulders.

"Now, we have to make sure that Lee doesn't discover that you're still alive." Jack wanted to make sure she stayed safe.

"That might be a problem," Emily remarked slowly.

"Why would that be a problem if Liz stays hidden?" Jack asked wondering just what was going on.

"If it was Lee that broke in the other night, he could have discovered his mistake." Emily picked up her glass and took a long drink.

"Do you mean he could have found Tonya's driver's license?"

"Yes, he also took all our credit cards, my driver's license, and hers." Liz said quietly suddenly feeling very let down.

"I should have thought of that," Jack remarked leaning back and crossing his legs.

"Lee was here yesterday wanting to buy the house. Do you think he knows Liz is still alive?" Emily couldn't wait for this all to be over.

"I have a feeling he probably does. Liz, when Emily isn't here, you should be sure to hide."

Smiling, Emily said, "We have that covered." Turning to Liz, she asked, " Shall we show him?"

Standing up, they said in unison, "Follow us."

Curious, Jack followed the pair upstairs. They took him into a bedroom and proceeded to open the closet. Liz went to the back of the closet and moved her foot along the base of the back wall. Suddenly the wall opened. Emily took a flashlight and motioned for him to follow them. Jack was surprised at what he saw. It was a hidden room. The room contained a couch and a small table.

"There's more," Emily said leading the way. "Be careful, the stairs are very old."

Jack followed Liz and Emily down the stairs. They came to a wall. Emily moved her foot along the base of the wall and triggered a mechanism that opened another secret door. They found themselves in the broom closet in the kitchen.

"This is quite a house." Jack just shook his head in total disbelief. "How did you discover that secret room?"

"I guess one of the advantages of spending a lot of time in the attic over the garage was I had a lot of time on my hands. There was an old trunk up there along with a lot of old papers. I discovered a book that told the history of this house along with the history of the town. While reading it, we read about the secret room and checked it out for ourselves."

"Liz said there are a lot of interesting things about this house that she read about."

"Yeah, like this house used to be a bordello. They would use the secret room to hide influential men who didn't want it to be known that they frequented a house of ill repute."

"This just keeps getting better and better," Jack said laughing.

"And actually these stairs used to lead to the outside. In later years the kitchen was made bigger and the porch added on."

"I think that's about enough history for me tonight. I had better go, so I can contact my friend. I'll keep in touch with you and make sure you don't have any problems." Jack told them good night and was about to leave. Stopping he turned with a puzzled look on his face. "There is one thing that is nagging at me, Liz."

"What's that?" Liz remarked, quietly, hoping he wasn't having a change of heart.

"Emily told me that you hated sleeping pills."

"That's right."

"Then why did you have a bottle if you didn't like them?" Jack asked trying to make sense of this.

"A couple of years ago I had an accident in which I sprained my ankle. At that time I was having trouble sleeping, so my doctor prescribed sleeping pills. I got the prescription filled, but never took any." Liz was wondering if he would believe her explanation.

"Why didn't you just throw them away?"

"I don't know? I just never thought about it. When I moved here I was in such a hurry I just through everything together and didn't really think about it. You do believe me, don't you?" Liz looked pleadingly at Jack.

"I believe you, Liz," Emily remarked putting her arm around Liz's shoulder. "I'm sure Jack does too, right, Jack?" Emily looked at Jack waiting for him to respond.

"Of course I believe you. I've had things in my medicine cabinet for years not even remembering that they were there." Smiling Jack took Liz's hand and gave it a squeeze. "Now, I better get going so I can get this information into the right hands." Jack quickly went out the door and to his car.

"I am so glad that Jack knows everything," Emily said as she and Liz walked back into the living room.

"So am I. He seems to know the right people." Liz picked up her glass of tea and sat down on the couch.

"He really does. It makes you wonder who Jack Baker really is."

Chapter Eleven

"So, what did you find out about the ever helpful Jack Baker?" Lee asked when Jeff came back from town.

"Well, it looks like he has moved out of the Willow Tree."

"Jack has decided to leave town," Lee remarked, sitting down at his desk.

"I don't think he's left town, boss," Jeff said taking out a little notebook from his pocket.

"I thought you said he moved out of the Willow Tree. If he didn't leave town, then where did he go?"

There was a knock on the door before Jeff could continue. "Come in," Lee called.

"I was just wondering if you had made any plans for taking care of our situation," Michael commented, sitting in one of the leather chairs in front of Lee's desk. "I'm getting kind of bored just sitting around here all day."

"I can give you plenty to do if you're that bored. There's

always something to do around the ranch. Isn't that right, Jeff?"

"Yeah, there's always plenty to do in the barns with the horses." Jeff chuckled.

Michael just stuck his nose up in the air. "Barns and horses are not my thing. I'm more the planning type."

"Well plan on shutting up so that Jeff can give me a report of what Jack Baker is up to," Lee grumbled, becoming very annoyed with Michael's whining.

With everyone quiet, Jeff continued. "Jack moved out of the Willow Tree and rented an apartment in town."

"Sounds like he's planning on staying awhile. Did you find out anything else?" Lee wasn't happy that Jack was going to be around for a while. He preferred him out of the way, but he'd deal with him if necessary.

"He spent a great deal of time with Emily last night at Liz's place."

"I don't like the idea of the two of them becoming so chummy. That can't be good for us." Lee got out of his chair and walked over to the window.

"There is one other thing, boss," Jeff said closing his notebook and putting it back in his pocket.

"What other wonderful news do you have for me?" Lee turned around and stood with his back to the window.

"Jack was seen leaving town this morning."

"Was there anyone with him?"

"No, he was by himself."

"If he just moved into an apartment, he didn't leave for good. Like a bad penny I'm sure he'll be back. Did you find out anything else about him? What he does for a living? Where he's from?"

"Sorry, boss, there just doesn't seem to be much out there about this guy."

"Thanks."

Lee sat back down in his chair and motioned for Jeff to leave the room. He sat quietly just thinking. Jack was becoming more annoying all the time. Who was he, and what was he doing in Hampton?

"So, what's your plan?" Michael asked, breaking the silence.

"I think I'm going to pay another visit to Maggie. Jack has stayed at the Willow Tree every time he's been in town. I've done some checking of my own, and it seems like he has been here quite often over the last year."

"Do you think the two of them are having a little fling, if you know what I mean?" Michael said draping his leg over the arm of the chair.

"I think she knows a lot about Jack Baker, and I'll just have to see how willing she is to give me any information."

"What if she isn't willing to talk?"

"Well then, I'll just have to do a little persuading to get the information out of her." Lee got up, put on his hat and went to the door.

"Do you want me to come with you?" Michael asked getting out of the chair.

"No, you idiot. Maggie thinks you left town, and I want to keep it that way," Lee remarked angrily.

"So what am I supposed to do?" Michael whined.

"Read a book or something. Just stay here and keep quiet." Lee opened the door, slamming it shut behind him. "Geez, I'm surrounded by morons."

Lee sat in his truck watching the Willow Tree. He hoped Maggie would cooperate and give him the information he wanted about Jack and Emily. She was a friend with both so she had to know what was going on. Stepping out of his truck, Lee placed his cowboy hat on his head and went up to the porch of the Willow Tree.

Maggie heard the door open and called out, "I'm in the dining room."

Lee stood leaning against the doorjamb waiting for Maggie to turn around. Too bad she had become a prude when he came into his money and broke off their engagement. She had brains, but she was too honest.

"May I help you?" Maggie said wiping her hands and turning around. "Oh, its you." She turned back to continue dusting the china cabinet.

"Why, Maggie, that hurt," Lee remarked. " I thought we were friends."

"Were is the operative word here. You haven't been by here the entire time that I have owned the Willow Tree, and now you come by twice in just a few days." Maggie picked up a porcelain egg that was sitting on the china cabinet and carefully began dusting it.

Lee came up beside her and grabbed the egg from her. "You know, Maggie, we can do things the easy way, or we can do them the hard way." He tossed the egg in the air just barely catching it. He continued to do this to see how Maggie would react.

Maggie was about to say something about how expensive the egg was, but she kept quiet knowing that any comments she made would just feed into Lee's rude behavior. "What is it you want, Lee?"

"When we talked the other day, I told you that I wanted you to get information about what Jack and Emily were up to. So what can you tell me?" Lee continued throwing the egg up in the air, and just barely catching it.

"There isn't anything to tell. Jack and Emily haven't told me anything. I have no idea what they are up to, and even if I did, I wouldn't tell you."

The egg crashed to the floor. "Oops," Lee remarked with a shrug.

Maggie wanted to slap him, but she restrained herself for the moment.

"Now, Maggie," Lee said moving closer to her. "That wasn't a very nice thing to say. If I didn't know better, I'd think you didn't like me very much. That's not very nice, especially since we were engaged at one time."

Maggie had her back to the china cabinet and couldn't move anywhere because Lee was right in front of her. She could see that he was becoming angry. He didn't like it when people stood up to him.

"You know, Maggie, I could have you shut down just like that," Lee said, snapping his fingers. "Just keep crossing me, and that is exactly what I will do."

His face was just inches from hers. She could see the evil in his eyes, and it made her blood run cold. She had made a very bad enemy. "I guess you will just have to do what you have to do," Maggie whispered trying to hold herself together.

Putting his finger under her chin, he lifted her head so that she had to look at him. His other hand was clamped to her arm squeezing it. In a low whisper he said, "You know I take whatever I want in this town, my Sweet Maggie." He brushed her lips with his.

She pushed him away and pulled her arm out of his grasp. She wiped her mouth with the back of her hand in disgust.

Lee was about to grab her again when he was pulled away. "I don't think so," the gentleman said.

Maggie and Lee were both surprised to see someone standing there. They hadn't heard him come in.

"This is no concern of yours," Lee growled, reaching out to take a hold of Maggie's arm.

"When I see a female being abused by a bully, I think it is."

Lee took a swing at him and missed. The gentleman hit him in the stomach causing Lee to double over in pain.

"It looks like you're not such a big man when you have someone your own size to pick on. Now I think you had better go." With that he escorted Lee to the door and watched him as he got in his truck and left.

Maggie stood in the doorway of the dining room rubbing her arm and watched him take care of Lee. She was very grateful for his showing up when he did.

"Are you all right?"

"Yes, thank you. I don't know what would have happened if you hadn't come in."

"I'm just glad I was at the right place at the right time. Clyde Thornton's my name." He held out his hand.

Maggie shook it and tried to smile. "I'm Maggie." She tried to take a few steps but was kind of wobbly. She would have fallen if Clyde hadn't caught her.

"Let me help you to the chair." He led her over to one of the dining room table chairs and then sat in the chair next to her.

Maggie was beginning to gain her composure. She smiled at Clyde and noticed the most beautiful blue eyes she had ever seen. They were soft and twinkled when he smiled at her. She could feel herself blushing.

"Do you have any rooms?" Clyde asked, breaking the spell.

"Yes, I do." Why don't you follow me to the other room, and I can get you registered.

"Are you sure you're up to it?" Clyde asked still showing concern for Maggie.

"I'm fine now." Maggie got up and led the way. She walked around her desk and got a card for Clyde to fill out. She felt an attraction to him, but dismissed it as infatuation due to his coming to her rescue. He had long brown hair that was pulled back in a ponytail. He had a scruffy beard and his clothes were crumpled. Not someone she would normally take a second look at.

"There you go," Clyde remarked handing the card and pen

to Maggie.

She handed him the key. "I'll show you to your room." Maggie led the way upstairs. "I put you in the rose room. It has its own bathroom. The other rooms on that floor share a bathroom."

"I appreciate having the privacy of my own bath."

"Here we are." Maggie stepped aside so that Clyde could unlock the door.

"Thanks." Clyde smiled at her and then went into his room.

Maggie was surprised by her reaction. She figured it was all just part of the encounter she had with Lee and Clyde's having been the one to help her.

The rocks were flying behind the pickup as Lee sped down the road to his ranch. He had had enough. He slammed on the brakes and stopped just inches from his garage door. Getting out of the truck, he took off in the direction of the barn without even closing the door.

Saddling up his horse, Mustang, he took off toward the wooded area on his property. He rode Mustang hard until they were both out of breath. The wind blowing in his face helped him calm down. Slowing his horse to a walk, he let himself rock gently with his horse. He stopped when they came to a small stream. Sliding off of Mustang he led him to the water so he could drink. Lee knelt down cupping his hands, and took a drink of the cool, clear water. Leaving Mustang by the water, Lee walked over and sat under a nearby tree.

"No one stands up to Lee Masters and gets away with it," he thought. They would pay. Starting with Emily. He knew Liz was hiding out in the house with her. Their time was coming, and they would pay dearly for trying to get him into trouble. When he was finished taking care of Emily and Liz, then the rest would pay, and he was going to enjoy every minute of their downfall.

Back at the barn, Lee fed Mustang and brushed him until his coat shone. He put him back in his stall and went into the house.

"So, did you have a talk with Maggie? Did she give you any information about Emily and Jack?" Michael asked Lee as he walked into his office.

"Didn't you even move while I was gone?" Lee asked in disgust. He went around his desk and sat down.

"Sure, I moved. I had to go to the bathroom," Michael laughed.

Lee just looked at him. "Shut up."

"You seem to be in a bad mood. Maggie didn't give you any information? Shot you down, huh." Michael put his hands behind his head.

Lee pounded his fist on the desk. "If you know what's good for you, you'll get out of here right now."

Michael didn't need to hear any more. He knew he had pushed Lee too far. He was out of the room in a flash.

Jeff had heard him shouting at Michael and was reluctant to knock on the door. He knew though that Lee would want to have this new information. Taking a deep breath and then holding it, he knocked on the door.

"It better not be Michael knocking," Lee shouted.

"It's me boss, Jeff,"

"Come on in, Jeff. Sorry to shout at you. Michael is becoming very annoying."

"I just wanted to tell you that Jack is back in town. My sources saw him return to his apartment about a half hour ago."

"Did your sources say if he stopped by Emily or Maggie before going to his apartment?"

"As far as they know, he went directly to his apartment."

"Thanks. You can go."

He'd like to send Michael packing, but he was going to help him with his plan to get rid of Emily and Liz. Getting up from his desk, he walked to the door and opened it. Shouting, "Michael, get your ass in here if you know what's good for you." He sat back down and waited.

"I knew you couldn't stay mad at me," Michael said grinning.

"Sit down and shut up." Lee stood up and walked over to the window, and for once Michael didn't make a comment. "We are going to discuss my plan for taking care of Emily and Liz. And," Lee said turning around and facing Michael. "I don't want you to say a word. Understood?"

Michael kept his mouth shut and just nodded.

Maggie was working in the kitchen when Clyde Thornton came downstairs. He came into the kitchen and sat at the island watching Maggie as she worked. "You look like you enjoy what your doing."

Maggie jumped at the sound of his voice and quickly turned around to see who was there.

"I'm sorry, I didn't mean to startle you."

"That's okay. I guess I'm still a little jumpy from my run in with Lee." Maggie turned around and finished brushing the melted butter over the cinnamon rolls. She put them in the oven and washed her hands. Maggie noticed that Clyde had trimmed up his beard and put on clean clothes that weren't crumpled.

"He doesn't seem like a very nice person."

"He isn't. Would you like a glass of iced tea?" Maggie went to the refrigerator and took out a pitcher of tea. She filled a glass and sat it in front of Clyde and then poured one for herself.

"He seems to enjoy hurting women. By the way, how's your arm?" Clyde took a sip of his tea.

Maggie set a plate of homemade cookies on the counter in front of Clyde. "My arm's fine, but it isn't just women. He doesn't like anyone who stands up to him, man or woman."

"I think he needs someone to take him to task for his outburst today. Maybe you should call the police and press charges against him." Clyde picked up a cookie and took a bite. "Mmmm. These are delicious."

"Thank you." Maggie sat on the stool across from Clyde. "It wouldn't do any good talking to the police."

"Why's that?"

"He owns the police in this town. No one stands up to him because they know it wouldn't do any good. If they go to the police with their concern, they just ignore it or twist it around so that the person complaining looks like the guilty party."

"He sounds like a very mean person. I always say what goes around comes around. And one of these days, things will change, and he'll get what's coming to him."

"You sound pretty sure of yourself."

"With those types, eventually they do. Sometimes it doesn't happen fast enough, but they get theirs." Clyde took another cookie and took a bite. "They sure are good."

Smiling, Maggie got up to check on her cinnamon rolls. They needed just a few more minutes before they were done.

"Those cinnamon rolls sure smell good."

"You're going to have to wait until breakfast to try one." Maggie turned off the oven and took the rolls out and set the pan on a wire rack to cool.

"I think I'm going to stretch my legs. Thanks for the tea and the delicious cookies." Clyde got up and walked to the kitchen door and stopped. "I'm looking forward to having those cinnamon rolls for breakfast." Turning, he left the room.

Maggie heard the front door open and then close. Clyde Thornton was a very interesting man she thought mixing up the frosting for the rolls.

"I hope I don't have to go over this again," Lee said, leaning back in his chair.

"I got it," Michael said quietly. "You don't have to go over it again."

"Good. So that is the way we are going to take care of Emily and Liz. With them out of the picture, no one can prove anything." Lee put his hands behind his head turning his chair to look out the window.

"I'm going to go and get some fresh air." Michael got up and headed toward the door.

"You do that and stay out of trouble." Lee heard the door close and shook his head. Michael was such an idiot. Getting out of his chair, Lee walked over to the window. Looking at the horses in the field, he chuckled to himself. "It won't be long now."

Chapter Twelve

"That was Jack," Emily said putting her cell phone in her pocket. "He said he's working on a couple of things and will be by tomorrow when things are more finalized."

"I will be so glad when this is over and Lee is in jail." Liz put the last box on the shelf in her closet. "I don't know how much more my nerves can take."

"We'll get through this. When everything settles down, I think the two of us need to take a little vacation."

"That sounds like a good idea. Just get away for awhile." Liz smiled and picked up the step stool and moved it out of the closet.

"Look what I kept out," Emily said holding up a couple of photo albums.

"I haven't looked at them in ages. Let's take them downstairs and look through them." Liz closed the closet door, and they went down to the living room.

Sitting on the couch Emily, began paging through the album. Liz sat down next to her. They really had a lot of fun in high school.

"Oh my, look at those hairdos and the dresses. Neither one of us had dates for our Junior Prom, but we went and had fun." Emily laughed turning the page.

"This brings back so many happy memories," Liz remarked feeling a little bit sad also. The innocence of those days for them changed very quickly when they went away to college.

"College was a different story wasn't it?" Emily said seemingly reading Liz's mind.

"When does all the tragedy stop?"

"Unfortunately tragedy doesn't stop, so you have to focus on the happy times to help even things out." Emily put her arm around Liz and gave her a squeeze.

"I guess you're right. I had been focusing on the happy times these last few years, but the recent events have started the tragic memories to come tumbling back."

"Together we'll get through this and focus on our happy memories." Emily closed the album.

"I'm sure glad you're here to help me through all this." Liz took the album and placed it on the coffee table. Turning to Emily, she said, "You know what I'm hungry for?"

"I haven't the slightest idea."

"Ice cream," Liz said laughing. "Whenever we were feeling down, we'd always go and have ice cream."

"We did, didn't we? I can go get us some."

"But you can't get two of them. Someone might wonder who you were getting it for."

"I can get a large, and we can share it. No one would think that is fishy. They might think I'm a pig, but that's okay."

Liz just laughed. "No one is going to think you're a pig. I'll go upstairs to the secret room while you're gone." She picked up the album and headed upstairs.

Emily waited a couple of minutes to make sure she had enough time to get into the room. Picking up her purse, she went to her car to get some ice cream.

The place was busy. It was a warm June evening, and people were out enjoying themselves. Emily placed her order and waited for her ice cream. She quickly left after getting her order. Getting back into her car, she went back to the house. She had her window down and could feel the gentle breeze against her cheek as she drove. The setting sun painted the sky a beautiful pink, purple, and yellow. The fingers of the sunlight through the few clouds filled the sky. How she wished they could sit outside on the swing and enjoy this lovely evening. Soon they would be able to, hopefully really soon.

"I have our ice cream," Emily said opening the secret door.

"Let's go eat," Liz stated, pulling the door closed behind her and closing the closet door.

They went down to the kitchen to get another spoon. They sat at the dining room table sharing their treat.

"This tastes so good, " Liz remarked, taking another spoonful.

"Hey now, don't take it all! I want my share too." Emily laughed and pushed Liz's spoon out of the way so that she could take another bite.

Putting her spoon down, Liz said, "I just remembered a room that needs to be straightened up from the break-in."

"I thought we took care of all of them."

"My darkroom is a mess. I saw it yesterday when I went to get the memory card for Jack." Liz quickly took another bite while Emily sat thinking.

"As soon as we finish this, why don't we take care of the darkroom so that everything is done?" Emily took a bite and pushed the cup to Liz so that she could finish it.

Liz took the last bite and threw the cup away in the wastebasket in the kitchen. "Let's get it done."

Emily turned on the light in the darkroom and saw what Liz was talking about. Pictures that she had developed were thrown all over. Some of them were torn. Bottles tipped over. Some were dumped in the trays and in the sink. Things from the drawers were thrown all over and the drawers pulled out.

"I'll get a trash bag, so we can just throw away everything that's not any good." Emily went to the broom closet and got a trash bag. She returned, and they started cleaning up.

"These pictures are ruined," Liz said holding up several that she picked up off the floor. She placed all of them in the trash bag. The negatives she picked up and placed on a shelf. When she had time, she would try to see if they could still be used.

Before long they had the room back in shape. Emily tied the trash bag shut. "I'm going to take this out and put it in the garbage can."

"Can I do that? It's dark outside, and I would just love to get some fresh air." Liz wanted to go out so badly. She was so tired of being cooped up.

"I don't think that would be a good idea. If Lee has someone watching the house, and they would see you, we would be in trouble. I know it's hard, but it will soon come to an end." Emily carried the trash bag to the kitchen.

"I know you're right. I'll wait for you in the living room." Liz went and sat on the couch trying not to feel dejected.

Emily turned on the porch light and went down the steps to the garbage cans. Lifting the lid, she pushed the bag down into the can.

"Hello, Emily."

Emily jumped and turned around. She opened her mouth to scream to warn Liz, but Lee quickly put his hand over it. Her eyes got big at the sight of the gun he had pointing at her.

"Now don't do anything stupid. Let's get inside." Lee motioned Michael to go first.

Emily figured she could yell at Liz to run when they got inside. Lee must have figured the same thing because he shoved the gun into her back and clamped his hand over her mouth.

Liz came walking over to the kitchen when she heard the door. She stopped short when she saw Michael. Emily and Lee were right behind him.

Once inside Lee chuckled. "Well, well, who have we here? Liz has come back from the grave only to be gone again." He took his hand off of Emily's mouth and shoved her in Liz's direction.

"You were right, Lee. You said she was hiding out in the house."

Michael stood next to Lee and pointed his gun at Liz and Emily. "We got'em now."

"Shut up, Michael," Lee snapped. "Why don't we all go into the living room so we can have a little chat."

Emily and Liz turned around and went into the living room. They sat down on the couch and took each other's hand and sat quietly.

"Now," Lee said, pulling up a chair and sitting right in front of Liz and Emily. The only thing that separated them was the coffee table. "Let's chat."

"We have nothing to talk about, so you might as well leave," Emily said bravely.

"She's not too smart, is she Lee?" Michael remarked standing next to him.

"Sit down and shut up, Michael."

Michael quietly sat on the chair next to the couch.

Lee didn't say anything for what seemed like an eternity. He just sat glaring at the two of them.

"Why don't I make us some tea," Emily said, getting ready to stand up.

"Sit down. You two are really starting to annoy me, and I

don't like to be annoyed." Lee stood up, reaching across the coffee table, and grabbed Liz's arm, pulling her to her feet. "Now, you have something I want, and you better give it to me."

Liz chewed on her bottom lip trying to keep the tears from falling. She didn't want to give Lee the satisfaction of seeing her cry.

"I want those pictures, and I want them now." Lee was just inches from Liz's face. "Where are they?"

"Leave her alone," Emily shouted jumping up next to Liz.

"Shut up," Lee said, pushing her back down on the couch. Glaring at Liz, he said. "Are you going to get me those pictures?"

Liz just nodded her head.

"Liz is coming with me, and Michael will stay here with you, Emily," Lee said turning to look at her. "And Liz is going to get those pictures I want. And if you don't," Lee said pulling on Liz's arm so that she had to face him, "Michael will kill Emily, and we will put the blame on you. So if you value your friendship, you'll do as I say."

"I'll make sure Emily stays right where she is," Michael said moving over to the couch and sitting next to her.

"So where do you have the pictures?"

"Upstairs on the third floor," Liz whispered trying not to wince in pain from Lee squeezing her arm.

"Let's go upstairs." Lee jerked her arm, and the two of them went to the third floor.

"How can you let Lee get away with this? He had your sister kidnapped and taken to Mexico for who knows what purpose." Emily was trying anything to reason with Michael.

"You know what? There was no love lost between Julia and me. She always thought I was scum. I was finally making good money, and she had to stick her nose in and try to mess it up."

"I don't understand how anyone could let something like that happen to someone in their own family whether you got along or not!" Emily just shook her head, knowing that if he let that happen to his own sister, Michael wouldn't lift a finger to help them. Things seemed very hopeless at the moment, but she had to stay calm and think. The cold metal on her arm made her jump.

"You know, we could have a little fun while Lee and Liz are upstairs, if you know what I mean." Michael whispered in her ear.

Liz and Lee got up to the turret room. Lee looked around not seeing where she could have hidden anything. "Are you trying to provoke me?" he said, pushing her away from him. She stumbled and almost fell. "There's nothing in here. Now you better show me where those pictures are or I will shoot you here on the spot." Lee pointed the gun at Liz.

"They're here if you just let me show you," Liz remarked, trying to calm herself.

"You better make it quick, and this better not be a joke because I don't like jokes." Lee lowered the gun.

Liz ran over to the far wall and ran her hand along the molding. She was nervous and having trouble finding the spring to open the drawer.

"If you think this is going to buy you time, you're sadly mistaken."

"There's a secret drawer here. I just have to find the little spring under the molding so that the drawer comes open." She continued feeling along the bottom of the molding. Finally she found the spring and opened the drawer. Taking out the envelope, she handed it to Lee.

"It's about time," Lee said taking the pictures out of the envelope and looking at them. "Let's get back downstairs. He pushed Liz ahead of him, and they went back down.

Hearing their footsteps coming down the stairs, Michael went back and sat on the chair next to the couch.

"Liz was very cooperative," Lee said holding up the envelope with the pictures. "Now all I need are the negatives, and then we can have a little party to celebrate.

"I don't have any negatives," Liz said quietly.

"Don't give me that. All pictures have negatives." Lee was once again becoming very agitated.

"I took the pictures with a digital camera. You just hook the camera up to a computer, and that's how you make the pictures." Liz left out the part about the memory card since she had given it to Jack.

"Then get me the camera," Lee said shoving the gun in her face.

"The camera is in my darkroom."

"Let's go."

Liz went past the stairs, down the little hallway. She opened the door at the end of the hall and turned on the light. She picked up the camera that was on the table and handed it to Lee.

"Now back to the living room, so we can have that party." Lee put the envelope on the coffee table and set the camera on top.

Michael got up, and Liz sat back down next to Emily. "Let's see what you got there," Michael said reaching for the envelope.

"For one thing, we have this," Lee grabbed the gun out of Michael's hand and shot him before Michael even realized what Lee was doing.

Emily and Liz jumped at the sound the gunshot. They were terrified at what they had just witnessed. They both stared at Lee in horror at what he had done. "Why?" Emily and Liz said in unison.

"All just part of my little plan." Lee sneered at Michael's body and kicked him with his boot to make sure he was dead, dropping the gun next him.

"Don't you think someone might have heard the gunshot?" Emily asked, finally finding her voice.

"Naw, this house is really very isolated for being in town. The only house even close is Miss Nosy Pants across the street, and she doesn't worry me."

"But if she sees your vehicle, she might come over." Emily hoped with all her heart that she would.

"But my vehicle isn't outside. We came in Michael's car, and we parked down the street so we wouldn't be seen."

Emily's heart sank when she heard those words. She didn't know what they were going to do. She looked at Liz and just wanted to cry, but she knew she had to be strong. If she let go, so would Liz, and they needed to stay calm and think clearly right now.

"So, what happens now?" Emily asked taking Liz's hand and giving it a squeeze.

"First, you're going to pick up that gun," Lee said pointing to the one next to Michael's body.

"Why?"

"You sure do ask a lot of questions. Because you killed Michael, and you left town because you didn't want anyone to find out what you did. Now pick up the gun."

Emily had never touched a gun in her life, and she was terrified to pick it up. She walked over to the body and slowly reached down to pick up the gun. She realized that she had a gun and could shoot Lee. Raising the gun, she pointed it at Lee.

He just started laughing. "Do you think I'm stupid? There was only one bullet in that gun, and it was for shooting Michael. Believe me, I wouldn't have you pick up a loaded gun."

Emily felt hopeless. She lowered the gun.

"Now drop it next to Michael and go sit back down."

Emily did as she was told. Sitting back on the couch, she took Liz's hand. "So what happens now?"

"You two are going to disappear just like Julia did. People already think Liz is dead so that won't be a problem, and you, like I said before, it'll look like you left town after killing Michael."

"You sure don't seem to have a problem killing people who get in your way."

"I run this town, and I take care of anyone who thinks they can take me down. I don't care who it is." Lee moved the curtain to look out. Jennifer Brack's car was in the driveway, but her house was completely dark. "Let's go."

Emily and Liz walked slowly toward the front door. Lee picked up Emily's purse and keys and threw them at her. "You're driving out to my ranch. Now let's move." He pushed them both causing them to stumble into each other and almost fall. "Come on." Lee grabbed Emily's arm and opened the door.

She almost screamed out in pain, but managed to bite her lip to keep from doing so. She was afraid he would have shot them both right there. There was no one in sight as they came out onto the porch.

Lee quickly shuffled them to the car. He pushed Liz into the back seat while Emily went around to the driver's side. He then got in the back seat next to Liz.

"Now don't try anything funny, or Liz here will get it for sure, and this time she won't come back from the dead."

Emily knew he was serious. Putting the car in reverse, she backed out of the driveway and headed in the direction Lee told her.

Jennifer pushed back the curtain in her bedroom. Was that a gunshot she had heard? She didn't see anything; it must have been a car backfiring. Light was coming through the closed curtains in Liz's house. Emily was up late, but then it seemed like she usually was. Jennifer went back to bed.

The sound of a car starting had her jumping out of bed and going to the window. Now why would Emily be going somewhere this time of night?

Chapter Thirteen

Jack pulled over when he heard the sirens to let the police cars pass. He wondered where they were going so early in the morning. As he got closer to Liz's house, he saw that the police cars had stopped there. What was going on? He was worried that something happened to Emily and Liz. A policeman stopped him as he was walking up the sidewalk to the house.

"I'm sorry sir, you can't go in there."

"The person that lives in this house is a friend of mine. I need to know that she is all right." He was about to push past the officer when Detective Daniels came out on the porch. "Detective, can I talk to you?" Jack shouted.

Daniels motioned for him to come up on the porch. "What can I do for you?"

"I'm Jack Baker, and I'm a friend of Emily Jansen. What happened here?"

"It looks like your friend shot Michael Crawford and killed

him. Just like her friend Liz killed Julia Masters. Some friend you have there."

"How do you know that it was Emily?"

"We had an anonymous tip that there was a shooting and who did it. Plus her car is missing, and she is nowhere to be found." Daniels continued taking notes. "Now if you'll excuse me, I need to get back inside."

"Maybe it was self defense."

"I doubt it. The two knew each other. I think they were having a little tryst. Things got out of hand, and she shot him."

"So what evidence do you have supporting that supposition?" Jack wanted to get inside and look around for himself. Something definitely didn't feel right about this situation.

"I have everything I need to make that conclusion. He's dead in the house. She's gone, so what more do I need?" Detective Daniels turned to go back into the house.

"Do you mind if I look around?"

"Just don't get in the way."

Jack followed him into the house. In the living room Michael's body was covered with a sheet. He slipped upstairs to check out the turret room. When he got there, he noticed right away that the secret drawer was open, and the envelope was gone. Lee had been there, and he felt certain that he had Emily and Liz.

Stopping on the second floor, he checked out the bedroom where they were sleeping. All of Emily's things were still there. He closed the bedroom door and went to the closet. He managed to get the secret door open, but no one was inside. So Lee did have both of them. Back downstairs, he commented to Daniels, "You know that Emily didn't take any of her clothes with her. She really must have left in a hurry."

"That's what I figure." Detective Daniels continued taking notes.

"Thanks for letting me look around." Jack went back outside.

Detective Daniels followed him outside. "It looks like you need to do a better job of choosing your friends. You know the old saying, guilt by association."

"Oh, I know that old saying, and I've found that to be very true," Jack started going down the steps of the porch. He saw Jennifer Brack coming across the street.

Detective Daniels also saw her and remarked, "Do me a favor Baker and keep her away from here. All I need is for her to be nosing around."

Jack went down the sidewalk and intercepted Jennifer. Daniels watched as the two of them talked. They were speaking very quietly, so he couldn't hear what they were saying. Jennifer kept pointing toward the house, and Jack just shook his head. Daniels went back inside to see if his men had finished up. He would have to wait on the coroner to get there and pick up the body. Just as he was about to call again, he heard a vehicle pull up. When he went to the door, he saw that Jack and Jennifer had walked across the street and were still talking.

"Sorry I'm late," Doctor Barry, the coroner, remarked, coming up the steps. "I went out early to go fishing, and I drove back as soon as I got the call."

"The body's over here," Daniels said, leading the way. "I'll let you guys finish up, and I'm going to head back to the station."

Daniels went out to his car. He saw Jack get into his car. He was talking on his cell phone as he drove off. "I wonder what Lee thinks of this guy? He always seems to show up just like a bad penny," he thought getting into his car.

Jennifer watched from her window as they brought out the body and put it in the coroner's vehicle. The police closed up the house and left with the yellow tape fluttering in the breeze.

"So Michael didn't come back with you?" Jeff asked Lee as they went into his office.

"No, unfortunately Michael had a little accident and won't be back." Lee sat in the chair behind his desk. "The cargo is in the store room behind the kitchen. In the morning, we'll move it to the shed out by the airfield."

"Our contact called and left you a message."

"What was the message?" Lee asked, crossing his arms in front of him on his desk.

"They won't be able to get here until about six o'clock tomorrow night instead of one o'clock."

"Damn, I was hoping this would all be done by tomorrow afternoon. I guess a few extra hours won't make any difference. I want you to make sure everything is arranged with the boys. Just tell them the same as the last time."

"Sure thing. Do you want me to check on the cargo before heading out?" Jeff asked walking to the door.

"No, that's okay. I'll do that myself." Lee got up and went out with Jeff. He walked through the kitchen to the storeroom and opened the door. He chuckled to himself as he went inside.

Emily and Liz were bound and gagged leaning up against the wall. Lee walked over and crouched down in front of them. "Well, well. You two thought you could go up against Lee Masters and win. I don't think so." He stood up and walked to the door. Turning around, he said, "By this time tomorrow night, you will have new living accommodations in Mexico. When they get through with you down there, you'll wish you were dead." Laughing, he closed the door and went back to his office.

It was pitch black in the storeroom, but Emily scooted herself closer to Liz. When she bumped against her, she tried to get her to turn so that their backs could be together, and they could try to undo the rope that bound their wrists. After Emily bumped her a couple of times and turned, Liz realized what she wanted and did the same.

In his office, Lee stood by the window, looked out over the meadow and watched the horses grazing. He turned when he heard a knock on the door. "What is it?" he called.

"Boss, there's someone here that wants to see you," Jeff remarked quietly.

"Who is it?"

Jeff closed the door part way and said, "It's Jennifer Brack."

"What in the world does that fool woman want? Tell her I'm busy and can't see...."

Jennifer barged into the room before Lee could finish his sentence. "Lee Masters, you're just the person I wanted to see." She sat down in a chair in front of Lee's desk before he could even respond.

Breathing a deep sigh, Lee sat down at his desk and placed his hands in front of him. "What can I do for you, Miss Brack? I'm very busy, so just state what is on your mind and be on your way."

"Oh, I know you're a very busy man, but what I came out here for is very important to a lot of people." Jennifer looked around the room admiring the furnishings." "Very nice. You have excellent taste. Who was your decorator?"

"What is it you wanted to see me about?" Lee was getting very agitated by her presence.

"Oh yes, I wanted to ask you for a donation for our church. We are raising money to build a new playground for our preschool children. The one we have is very old, and the equipment is too dangerous for the children to play on."

Lee took out his checkbook and started writing. He handed her a check. "That should help you out. Now would you kindly leave?" He stood up, hoping that she would take the hint and stand up also.

Jennifer looked at the check and almost fainted at the amount he had made it out for. "Thank you very much, Mr.

Masters. This will almost take care of the rest of the money that we need." Slowly she got out of the chair as she put the check in her purse. Putting out her hand, she tried to shake hands with Lee who just turned and walked to the window. Undaunted, Jennifer continued, "Thank you again. Your check is greatly appreciated."

Jeff knew that Lee was getting madder by the minute, and that he had better get Jennifer out of there before he blew his stack. "Thank you, Jennifer," he said taking her by the arm and escorting her out of the room. "I'm sure your church will be very happy to see that check. So why don't you get back to town and show them." Jeff got her out of Lee's office and out the front door. He hurried her along to her car before she could say any more. Breathing a sigh of relief, he turned and went back into the house.

Lee heard Jeff come back into the room and turned, "Is Miss Nosy Pants gone?"

"Yes, she's gone. I'm really sorry about that boss. I didn't want her coming in here and bothering you."

"There was nothing you could have done to stop her. She was bound and determined to come in here, and she did just that." Lee just wondered why she showed up now. She wasn't just after a donation, but what was she after?

"I made sure that she headed out the way she came, and I called Bill to make sure she left the ranch and didn't turn down any roads she wasn't supposed to."

"Good thinking. Thanks for all your help." Lee turned and looked out the window. He loved watching his horses as they grazed in the pasture. Now back to business, he thought, turning from the window and taking out his cell phone. Chuckling, he pressed the numbers and put the phone up to his ear.

"So Detective Daniels, do you have any more information on the death of Michael Crawford and the disappearance of Emily Jansen?" Jack asked sitting in the chair in front of

Detective Daniels' desk. "Have you investigated the scene of the crime further for clues?" Jack knew he hadn't, but he wanted to antagonize him a little.

"I don't need to check things further. This case is all cut and dried, and when I find Emily Jansen, she will be convicted of Crawford's murder." Daniels leaned back in his chair and crossed his arms in front of him.

Daniels was so cocky, Jack felt like smacking him, but he refrained himself. "Do you think that is good police work just assuming something without any hard evidence. You know what they say when you ASSUME." Jack grinned at Daniels' discomfort by that remark.

"I'm not assuming anything. All the evidence points to Miss Jansen. Now, if you'll excuse me, I have work to do." Picking up a file, he got up from his desk and went into another room.

Jack followed right behind him. "So did you find Crawford's car? It wasn't parked at Liz's house."

"Yea, we found it parked a couple of blocks away." Detective Daniels continued to go through files.

"Wouldn't that indicate that maybe Crawford was up to no good and wanted to hurt Emily?" Jack crossed his arms in front of himself and leaned against the doorjamb just watching Daniels.

Slamming the file drawer shut, Daniels turned, clenching his fists in exasperation. "No, that just means that it was a clandestine meeting gone wrong." Daniels brushed passed him and went back to his desk.

Jack smiled to himself. He loved seeing Daniels fume. "Oh, so now you think they had a thing going, and she killed him because of...?"

"Because he was going to break up with her. Her hormones took over and bang," Daniels said pointing his finger at Jack.

Jack laughed and shook his head. "You've been reading too many romance novels, Daniels" He is such an idiot, he thought as he stepped out on the sidewalk.

"Hello," Jack said, grabbing his cell phone as he got into his vehicle. "You're going to take care of that?...I know, but that is very important....Okay, see you tomorrow."

"Are you all right?" Clyde asked as Maggie hung up the phone. She looked as white as a ghost.

"I can't believe I just agreed to have dinner with Lee Masters," Maggie commented shaking her head.

"Now why would you do something like that after the way he has treated you?" Clyde asked leaning against the doorway.

"I don't know," Maggie remarked shrugging her shoulders. "He said that he wanted to apologize for the way he acted." Turning to face Clyde, she continued, "I did tell him that I would meet him at the restaurant instead of his picking me up."

"Good move. That way you won't have to be alone with him." Clyde stuck his hands in his pockets quietly saying, "I could just happen to come in to have dinner about the time you meet Lee just to be around if you need assistance."

"You would do that?"

"No problem."

"I appreciate that," Maggie said with a sigh of relief.

Lee was waiting when Maggie arrived. The Maitre d' showed her to the table. He quickly got up and held the chair for her as she sat down. "Maggie, I'm so glad that you agreed to have dinner with me," Lee said, brushing her shoulder with his hand before sitting down opposite her.

Maggie cringed at the touch. It felt cold, and it took everything she had not to shiver. Trying to avoid eye contact at the moment, she picked up her napkin and put it on her lap and remarked, "You said you wanted to apologize, so I thought I owed you that much." Feeling a little more composed, she raised her head giving Lee a timid smile.

"I am very sorry for the way I acted the other day. It was very rude and boorish of me." Lee flashed her a big smile as he picked up his napkin and placed it in his lap. "I hope you accept my apology, and that we can be friends again."

With the arrival of the waiter, Maggie was able to avoid giving a response. She took the menu that was handed to her and began reading the items available.

"Would you like to see the wine list, Sir?" he asked Lee.

"No thanks. Just bring me the best bottle of champagne that you have. Tonight I'm celebrating," Lee said loud enough, so everyone around them could hear.

"What are you celebrating?" Maggie asked laying her menu on the table.

"I'm celebrating the fact that by tomorrow at this time an annoying problem that I've had will be taken care of, and I can sit back and enjoy my life again."

The waiter appeared with their champagne, and Lee didn't say any more. Maggie just wondered what he was talking about, but she wasn't about to ask any questions.

Lee handed a glass to Maggie and proceeded to make a toast. "To happy endings, especially for me." He clinked her glass and proceeded to take a big gulp of his champagne "Let's order." He signaled for the waiter and ordered the most expensive thing on the menu. "And the lady will have the same."

"Actually, I would rather have the Chicken Cordon Bleu," Maggie said looking at the waiter.

The waiter glanced at Lee before writing anything down. "You heard the lady; she wants the Chicken Condon Bleu."

"Very good." The waiter picked up the menus and left.

Clyde was seated at a table that hid him from Lee, but where he could observe what was going on. Lee seemed very confident. He must be getting ready to make a move. He saw Maggie get up from the table and head to the ladies' room. He got up and headed in that direction making sure Lee didn't see him. He touched her on the arm as she started to walk past him.

Maggie jumped, but was relieved to see that it was Clyde. "Hi."

"How's everything going?"

"Lee is acting very strange."

"How so?"

"He ordered champagne and is celebrating getting rid of a problem tomorrow."

"Did he say what the problem was that he was getting rid of?"

"No, he just said that by this time tomorrow a problem he had been having would be taken care of."

"You better get back before he wonders where you are."

"See you later."

Clyde took out his phone and made a call before going back to his table.

Lee stood up, came around the table and held Maggie's chair for her. "Thank you," she said quietly. Their dinner arrived, and she concentrated on her food, half listening to Lee brag about his money and all the things he owned. She just wanted the meal to end so she could go home.

"I hear the cheesecake is very good here. Shall I order some for us for dessert?" Lee asked, putting his fork on his plate and wiping his mouth with his napkin.

"No thank you. I am stuffed." Maggie put her napkin on her plate. "Thank you very much for dinner, but I really have to be going." She picked up her purse and pulled out her keys.

"So soon," Lee said dejectedly.

"I have a lot of things to do that can't wait until tomorrow." Maggie stood up and thanked Lee again for the dinner. She was about to leave when Lee reached across the table and grabbed her hand.

"We must do this again real soon." Lee rose from the table and with a sweeping gesture kissed her hand.

Maggie pulled her hand away and quickly left the restaurant. She was glad to be in her car. She didn't know what she had seen in him all those years ago.

Clyde finished his meal and sat watching Lee. He sure was full of himself, but not for long. After paying the check, Clyde left the restaurant. He needed to make a stop before he went back to the Willow Tree.

Lee met Jeff as he was walking into the house. "How has everything been tonight?" he asked, putting his keys in the dish on the table next to the door.

"Things have been quiet. Did you have a good dinner?" Jeff asked walking to the front door.

"I had a great dinner. The company could have been better. Tomorrow's a big day. I'll see you here bright and early."

"Good night." Jeff went out the door to where his truck was parked.

Lee closed and locked the door behind him. In his office, he poured himself a brandy. Maggie left in such a hurry he didn't have time to enjoy one at the restaurant. Setting the glass on his desk, he went out the door and down the hall to the storeroom by the kitchen. Opening the door, he turned on the light.

Emily and Liz both moaned at the bright light. It took a little time for their eyes to adjust to the brightness.

Lee laughed at their discomfort. "Tomorrow night at this time, you'll be having fun with some Mexican gentlemen. Actually, I don't know how gentlemanly they will be, but they'll be having fun. Good night." Switching off the light, he closed and locked the door.

Emily moved herself closer to Liz. They tried desperately to undo each other's hands. The more they tried, the worse it became until they gave up.

Chapter Fourteen

"Why don't you see if our two guests want something to eat," Lee said as he leaned against the counter in the kitchen.

"Should I bring them both in here or take food to them?" Jeff asked, taking off his gloves and laying them on the chair.

"We'll bring them in here. Only one at a time, that way they won't get any funny ideas of trying to escape." Lee turned around and opened the cupboard. Taking out a coffee cup, he poured himself a cup of coffee.

"Does it matter which one goes first?"

"No, it doesn't." Lee thought for a moment and said, "Actually, bring in Liz first. We'll let Emily stew a little by herself."

Jeff opened the door to the storeroom and turned on the light. Both Liz and Emily closed their eyes and turned their heads to avoid the bright light after being in the dark for so long.

"Okay, Liz," Jeff said walking over to where she sat on the floor. "Looks like you get to have a little breakfast." He reached down and helped her up. She was stiff from sitting so long and almost fell over. Jeff grabbed both her arms to steady her before walking her to the door.

Liz turned and looked at Emily, wondering just what was going on. She reluctantly let herself be led from the room. When they reached the kitchen, Lee was standing at the stove cooking eggs. The smell of the food made her realize just how hungry she was. The sound of the toast popping up caused her to jump. Lee and Jeff both laughed at her.

Lee turned the burner off and took the pan off the stove. "Untie her hands, and take the tape off her mouth. It would be a little difficult for her to eat otherwise. Besides I don't think she is going to try anything with Emily still locked up."

Jeff untied her hands and pulled the tape off her mouth and motioned for her to sit down. Liz sat in the chair indicated and rubbed her wrists. She could see red marks on them where the rope had rubbed her skin. Her face stung from the tape.

Lee set the plate of eggs and toast in front of her. "Eat."

After taking one bite, she put her fork on her plate. Even though she was hungry, it was difficult to swallow the food. She chewed and chewed but still had trouble swallowing.

"Here we try to do something nice, and she doesn't even appreciate it," Lee remarked sharply.

Finally getting the eggs down, Liz timidly asked, " Could I have some water to drink? I think that might help."

Lee motioned with his head, and Jeff got her a glass of water.

Liz took a long drink and set the glass on the table. She forced herself to eat the eggs and toast. She didn't want Lee to get mad and then not let Emily eat. She finished the last bite and placed her fork on her plate.

Emily sat in the dark storeroom wondering what was going

on. Why would they suddenly feed them? Hopefully they weren't hurting Liz. Whatever they had planned for them was happening today. That much she had gathered just from the brief comments Lee had made. She just wished she knew what they had planned. Had the police discovered Michael's body, and were they looking for her? Was Jack able to figure out what happened, and was he looking for her? She just had so many questions and no answers to any of them. Emily closed her eyes when she heard the door open. She didn't want to be blinded by the light.

Jeff flipped on the light and lead Liz over to where she had been sitting. Turning to Emily, he remarked, "Your turn." He reached down and helped her up making sure to hold on to her so she wouldn't fall.

Once in the kitchen, Jeff untied her hands and took the tape off her mouth. He indicated for her to sit in the chair by the table.

Emily was surprised to see Lee at the stove. The smell of the eggs and toast made her stomach growl. She realized that it had been quite some time since she had eaten.

Lee set the plate in front of her, along with a glass of water. "Eat." He stood by the counter with his arms crossed in front of himself and watched her.

Emily was self-conscious with Lee staring at her. She kept her eyes on her plate and ate the eggs and toast. Before she knew it, she had the entire glass of water gone. She had been thirsty. Once she had finished eating, Jeff tied her hands and put the tape back over her mouth.

"Soon, Emily. Very soon," Lee said taking her face in his hands. "You never should have messed with me." He laughed at the terror he saw in her eyes. Turning his back on her, he stared out the window as Jeff led her back to the storeroom.

What he had planned for them, Emily could not imagine. She hoped Jack knew that they just didn't leave town and was looking for them. Jeff helped her sit down next to Liz and then left them in darkness.

"So what's the plan?" Clyde asked Jack as he stepped into his living room. There was a map of Hampton plus one of the entire county that showed homesteads and ranches. There was a red circle around Lee's ranch.

"I have a couple more agents on the way, and I also contacted the state police."

"What time will the other agents and the state police get here?" Clyde looked over the county map. Lee had a pretty good spread. It would take some manpower to cover it all.

"The two agents will get here about one o'clock, and we'll just be meeting them outside of town and go over logistics. I'll be in contact with the state police via cell phone. I didn't want a lot of police coming into town causing a commotion and then have the locals alerting Lee."

"Do you really think that they are in cahoots with Lee?"

"I don't know if they are part of his organization, but he more or less tells them what to do, and they do it."

Clyde looked over the map and the area Jack had circled. Lee owned quit a spread. "Say, what's this small circle right here?" Clyde said, pointing to a circle at the far end of Lee's property.

Jack walked over to the table and looked over Clyde's shoulder at where he was pointing. "That is an old air strip. We figure that is how he gets his drugs in and out."

"Maybe that's how he gets rid of other cargo also."

"My thoughts exactly."

"It's time to move them to the shed at the air field." Lee picked up the keys to his truck and threw a set of keys to Jeff. "You take Liz in the jeep. Lay her on the seat and cover her with the tarp that's on the floor. I'll take Emily in my truck and put her in the back covering her with the tarp I have."

"Do you think it's necessary to cover them with a tarp? They'll get pretty hot under there."

"Yeah, I do. You never know what prying eyes might be around as we drive out the main gate. That nosey Jennifer could come back for more money for her church."

"Gotch ya." Jeff pulled a pair of gloves out of his pocket and put them on as they walked down the hall to the storeroom. "I'll go get the jeep and bring it around back by the kitchen."

"I'll wait till you get back before taking Emily out to the truck."

Jeff just nodded as he went out the door. He pulled out his phone when he got to the shed where the jeep was kept. After checking his messages, he slipped it back into his pocket and drove off toward the house.

Emily couldn't tell who was leaning against the doorjamb, just staring at them, without saying anything. It made her very uneasy. He hadn't moved since he opened the door. She wasn't sure how long it had been, but it seemed like an eternity. Glancing over at Liz, she was barely able to see her face. She could tell that her head was turned looking toward the door. Turning back to the door, he continued to just stand there without saying a word. She had a sickening feeling in the pit of her stomach that whatever they were planning on doing with her and Liz was about to happen. She heard footsteps fast approaching and then saw another man come into the doorway.

"Everything is all set, Boss," Jeff remarked taking off his gloves and standing next to Lee.

"Okay, then let's do it." Lee flipped on the light and walked over to Emily.

His evil smile caused her blood to run cold. There was no doubt in her mind that this was it. He wasn't planning on letting them go. She just knew that they would never be heard from again. She and Liz needed a miracle, and they needed one now.

Reaching down, Lee grabbed Emily's arm and pulled her to

her feet. He grabbed her other arm, pulling her within inches of his face as he stared down at her. "In a couple of hours, you'll be gone, never to be heard from again," he said through clenched teeth. "Nobody messes with me and gets away with it. Nobody."

Without another word, Lee led Emily out of the storeroom and down the hall to his waiting truck. He lifted her onto the bed of the truck, ordered her to lie down and then covered her with a tarp.

Jeff put Liz on the back seat of the jeep and put a tarp over her. He really didn't like doing that because it was beginning to get pretty warm, but he would do what he was told.

Lee led the way driving fast on the sand road. He didn't care that Emily was in the back and getting bounced around. He wanted to get to the airstrip as quickly as he could to get them into the shed before anyone unforeseen showed up.

The flapping of the corner on the tarp helped get fresh air to Emily as she bounced around. She was finally able to reach the side of the truck with her feet so that she could try and brace herself so that she didn't move all over. It helped somewhat, but she still would bang her head on the floor of the truck when he took a bump too fast. Emily hoped that Liz was having a better ride.

Liz was ready to pass out from lack of air under the tarp. The seat she was on was fairly comfortable, but she had to get some air. With her mouth-taped shut, she only had her nose to breath through. She was on her back so the tarp rested on her face completely. Bringing her arms up, she was able to lift the tarp a little so that she could breath a little better. Her arms soon tired so that she had to put them down to rest. After a few seconds, she put them back up. Wherever they were going, she hoped they got there soon so that she could get this thing off of her.

Lee came to a screeching halt, causing Emily to roll and bang her head on the side of the truck. Before she knew what was happening, she heard the tailgate open and Lee threw the tarp off of her. He grabbed her legs and pulled her to the tailgate where he proceeded to pick her up and fling her over his shoulder. She tried to hit him in the back with her tied hands, but he just laughed.

She looked around and could see Liz being lifted out of a jeep. Emily tried to make eye contact with her, but Lee swung around to talk to the other guy, almost causing her to hit her head against a pole.

"Sorry about the rough ride," Jeff whispered as he stood Liz on the ground. Taking her arm, he led her over to where Lee was holding Emily.

Lee set Emily on the ground like she was a sack of potatoes. Losing her balance she fell. Luckily she landed on her bottom and didn't fall back and hit her already sore head.

Laughing, Lee bent over and roughly pulled the tape off of her mouth. "You won't get away with this," Emily stammered. "They'll soon figure out exactly what has been going on."

"Who are they?" Lee asked arrogantly. "The police in Hampton?" He threw his head back laughing. "They are my puppets. I tell them what to do, and they do it." Turning, Lee unlocked the shed and opened the door. "In a couple of hours, you two will be history, and no one will be the wiser."

"You can't just kill us and expect to get away with it. Someone will put things together and take you down." Emily was terrified of what Lee had in mind, but she wasn't about to show it now. She just hoped and prayed that Jack was looking for them and would find them before it was too late.

"Who said anything about killing you? What's in store for you and Liz is a fate worse than death. Where you're going after a couple of days, you'll wish I had killed you. Maybe you'll see Julia. I sent her to the same place. But then, she's probably dead by now." Grabbing Emily's arm, he pulled her inside the shed and made her sit on the dirt floor.

Lee pointed to the far corner of the shed for Jeff to put Liz. "You can take the tape off her mouth. Nobody can hear them way out here. Besides the plane will be here in a couple of hours, and then they'll be history."

"Ladies, enjoy these next two hours because then you're on that plane to Mexico." Lee shrugged his shoulders and closed the door, making sure to padlock it.

Emily could hear the two men talking outside. Pretty soon she heard one vehicle start and then a second. She waited a few seconds listening to see if there was any other sound.

"Liz, are you okay?" Emily called out in the dark.

"I'm fine. How are you?"

"Other than being a little banged up from the ride, I'm fine." Emily's eyes began to focus in the darkness of the shed. There was a little light filtering in through the gaps in the boards that covered the windows. She could just barely make out Liz's figure across from her.

"How are we going to get out of this?" Liz asked, trying to scoot herself up to a more comfortable position. "Do you think Jack will be able to find us before it's too late?"

"Yes, he will," Emily, said emphatically, trying to convince herself as much as she was trying to convince Liz. "He's onto Lee, and he'll rescue us. I know he will."

"I hope you're right," Liz remarked quietly.

Emily wanted to move closer to Liz, but she really didn't know what she might run into. She had noticed several things sitting on the ground and leaning up against the wall. They would just have to talk to each other to keep their spirits up.

"I'm really sorry about all this, Emily. This isn't what I had planned for us to be doing this summer." Liz tried to hold back the tears that welled in her eyes. She was grateful that it was dark, and Emily couldn't see her. "I was looking forward to the two of us working on the house and opening a Bed and Breakfast."

"None of this is your fault, Liz. We will be working on your house and making it into a Bed and Breakfast." Emily swallowed to get rid of the lump in her throat before she continued. "I know things look bad right now, but I know that before that plane leaves with us on it, Jack will be here. I know he will."

Jack spread the map out on the hood of the vehicle. The men looked over the areas that he had circled in red. "We need to stop the plane from taking off. From reports I've gotten, he sent his wife on a drug plane to Mexico never to be heard from again. My guess is that he plans to do the same with Emily and Liz. Our primary goal is to get those two out unharmed."

"So for that very reason, we are going in without the sirens," Clyde remarked stepping up next to Jack. "We want to take them by surprise. We don't want any of Lee's men alerting him before we can get to the airstrip."

Chapter Fifteen

"It's time to go," Lee said, sticking his phone in his pocket. "I just talked to the pilot, and he is about twenty minutes away. Round up two of the guys to meet us at the airstrip. The rest put on alert."

"Okay, boss. The horses are saddled and ready to go." Jeff commented, getting on his phone as they walked out the door.

"Good, let's go and get this done."

Jeff finished his conversation and swung himself up into the saddle. It would take less than ten minutes to get to the airstrip. Jeff rode his horse hard in order to keep up with Lee.

Emily heard the galloping of horses as someone approached and hoped and prayed that it was Jack. She really didn't want to find out what was in store for them in Mexico.

Lee and Jeff got off their horses and tied them to a nearby tree. They brushed the dust off of their pants and then headed to the shed.

"Well, ladies, it is almost time...." Lee turned around and threw his head back laughing. He let the door slam shut, but did not lock it again.

Emily's heart sank. She had hoped it was Jack coming to rescue them. There was still time, she told herself.

"Do you still think Jack will make it on time?" Liz whispered.

"Yes, I know he will," Emily remarked trying hard to stay positive.

A truck pulled up, and two more men got out. Each was wearing a holster with a gun in it. They walked over to where Lee and Jeff were standing waiting for the plane.

"The other four guys are covering the perimeter to make sure we don't have any intruders," Ed, one of the two men, remarked.

"Good. I don't expect any trouble, but you never know." Lee heard a plane approaching and turned in the direction of the sound. "In just a few more minutes, this will all be over, and things can get back to normal around here."

The men watched as the plane came in for a landing. It was just a small turbo prop, but it served the purpose for them. The plane hit the dirt and bounced with the wheels coming up off the ground. It touched down again and this time stayed on the ground and taxied to a stop.

Lee walked over to the plane and waited for the pilot. He stepped out onto the wing of the plane and jumped to the ground. They shook hands and then exchanged envelopes. Lee then turned and motioned for them to get their cargo.

Jeff and one of the other men opened the shed door. Jeff took Emily, and the other guy took Liz and led them out of the shed.

On seeing the plane Emily, began fighting with everything she could muster. Liz began doing the same thing. It caught the men by surprise, and for a split second they let go. Emily and Liz took off running toward the woods.

"Do I have to do everything myself?" Lee shouted running back toward the shed.

Emily and Liz couldn't run very fast because of their hands being tied. They were just about to reach the woods when they were overpowered.

"That was not a good thing to do," Jeff said, grabbing Emily's arm and dragging her back toward the plane. She almost fell a couple of times because her legs were wobbly from running, and she was out of breath.

"You won't get away with this," Emily remarked, breathing deeply.

"That's right," Liz said, adding, "You will pay for your crimes."

"Mighty big talk for someone who is about to be sent away never to be heard from again."

Lee stopped them half way to the plane. He backhanded them both across the face. "Don't you ever try anything like that again," he said through clenched teeth. "I don't have time for this." Stepping to the side, he added, "Now get them on that plane."

The sound of all terrain vehicles and a helicopter approaching made them stop in their tracks. Looking around, they saw at least four vehicles just about two hundred yards away. They also saw a helicopter coming their way.

"Get those two on board now." Lee shouted running toward the plane.

The pilot hurried back into the cockpit and started the engine. The two men managed to get Emily and Liz on board just as the four wheelers came into the clearing. The men ran to take cover.

Jack had seen them put Emily and Liz in the plane. He motioned for Clyde to move the helicopter in front of the plane to try and stop it from taking off. He knew they had to be the ones to stop the plane because it would just run over the four wheelers. Besides, the four wheelers were needed to stop the men on the ground.

Clyde pulled the helicopter in front of the plane, which swerved to the left to turn, but the wheel hit a rut causing it to sputter and stop. He quickly put the helicopter down, and Jack was out and running toward the plane. Clyde was right behind him wanting to make sure that Emily and Liz were all right.

When Jack reached the plane, he saw that the pilot was knocked out after hitting his head on the control panel. Clyde caught up to him and he ran to open the cargo door to make sure the ladies were okay.

The sound of gunfire made Jack take a moment to look over the situation by the shed. He saw that Lee was running to get on his horse. If he got too far into the woods they would have a hard time trying to find him. "I'm going after Lee," Jack shouted to Clyde. "We don't want that one to get away."

Lee was just swinging himself up into the saddle when one of the four wheelers spooked his horse, causing him to rear up and knock Lee to the ground.

Jack grabbed Lee, forcing him face down in the dirt. He rolled, swinging and kicking, causing Jack to lose his balance and fall.

Lee scrambled to his feet ready to take on Jack. He wasn't about to let this guy ruin things for him.

Jack got to his feet. "Okay, Lee, let's see what you've got." He clenched his fists and took a jab at Lee. He caught Lee's jaw with a right swing.

Lee stumbled backwards, but managed to stay standing. He could taste the blood in his mouth. This made him even angrier, and he came back swinging recklessly, missing Jack completely.

Jack took another swing and struck Lee's cheek. His head flew to the side, and Lee went down. Pulling out his handcuffs, Jack rolled Lee on his stomach, brought his hands behind his back and cuffed them. "You have a right to remain silent...."

Clyde checked to make sure Emily and Liz were okay. "I will be right back," he said and then went to tie up the pilot before he came to.

"All right, ladies, let's get you untied." Clyde proceeded to untie first Emily and then Liz.

"We're so glad to see you," Emily said rubbing her wrists. "Is Jack with you?"

"Yeah, he took off after Lee. We don't want that one to get away," he said helping Liz to her feet. "Let's get out of here."

Back on the ground, Emily and Liz hugged each other, both grateful to be alive. "I told you Jack would find us," Emily whispered in Liz's ear.

Clyde, Emily and Liz were walking toward the others when three police cars pulled into the clearing. Clyde called to one officer to go get the pilot. Lee was handcuffed and lying face down on the ground.

"I'm sure glad that you two are all right," Jack commented walking over to them.

"We are so grateful that you got here when you did. If that plane had taken off for Mexico, I don't know what would have happened." Emily held back the tears. She was afraid if she started crying she wouldn't stop.

"It's all over with now. These guys will be going away for a long, long time. Lee won't be able to get out of this one," Jack said, motioning for the officer to take him away.

"It's too bad that you weren't here to help Julia. Who knows what happened to her in Mexico," Liz commented, brushing a tear from her face.

"I wish we had been here then also," Jack said solemnly.

"It looks like things are wrapped up here. How about if we give the ladies a ride back to town in the helicopter?" Clyde asked.

"Would you ladies like a helicopter ride?" Jack asked with a smile.

Emily and Liz looked at each other and then turned back to him nodding their heads, "Yes." They were both feeling exhausted by the events of the last few days. The only thing either of them wanted right now was to go home and get cleaned up.

Jack handed each one a headset to wear. "This way we can talk to each other. Also, it helps with the noise."

Clyde started the helicopter, and it slowly lifted off the ground. They passed over the plane. "Our agents are on their way to go over the plane with a fine tooth comb."

The trip back to town was uneventful with no one saying much of anything. Clyde landed the helicopter at the small airport on the edge of town. From there they took Jack's car back to the police station.

"How will you be able to keep Lee in jail with the police in this town basically working for him? They'll find a way to get him out," Emily asked, feeling nervous about coming face to face with Lee again.

"Oh, you don't have to worry about that," Jack remarked glancing over his shoulder at Emily and Liz. "Everyone who worked for the police department including Detective Daniels has been replaced with state police officers until they can make new appointees to their positions."

Emily took Liz's hand and gave it a squeeze. They both were smiling from ear to ear. "That is just wonderful," Liz said, breathing a sigh of relief.

The police station was swarming with activity when they pulled up. "We just have a few things to finish up here, and then we can get the two of you home," Jack remarked as they got out of the car.

The officers inside the station were busy processing Lee's men. They would spend the night here and then be transported to a state facility while awaiting trial.

"I know my rights. I want my one phone call. I want to call my lawyer," Lee shouted from lock-up.

Emily and Liz just looked at each other and were glad he was behind bars.

"Why don't the two of you sit right over here while we finish up," Clyde said, indicating two chairs in front of a big brown desk. "This used to be Detective Daniels desk, but no more."

Jack and Clyde went back to lock-up to talk to Lee. When he saw the two of them, he began shouting and calling them every name under the sun. "Lee, you need to keep your mouth shut and listen," Jack said quietly.

"You won't be able to make any of this stick, and I'll be out of here in no time. The police here won't let anything happen to me." Lee grabbed onto the bars and glared at Jack and Clyde.

"First of all," Jack said with a smile. "Those police officers don't have their jobs any more, and, secondly, the state police run this department. Third, we have enough evidence to put you away for good. You won't be getting out. We have enough witnesses to make sure of that."

"I don't care what you say. I'll beat this, and you won't have anything."

"We have pictures of you putting Julia on board that plane and sending her to Mexico. Plus with Emily and Liz's testimony, they will lock you up and throw away the key." Jack stopped for a moment to answer his phone. Putting it back in his pocket, he motioned for Clyde to follow him. They could hear Lee cursing at them as they closed the door.

Emily and Liz turned to see whom Jack and Clyde went to talk to. They were surprised to see Jennifer standing there with another woman. Jack and Clyde came over to where the two were sitting, followed by Jennifer and the other woman.

"Oh, my goodness!" Liz exclaimed, jumping to her feet. "Julia, you're alive!"

"Jennifer told me that I have you to thank," Julia said, giving Liz a hug.

"I just did what anyone would have done," Liz remarked modestly.

Emily looked at Jack wondering just what was going on. "How?"

"After you showed me those pictures, we sent a couple of our agents to Mexico to do some digging. Yesterday, they found Julia tied up in a house that dealt in drugs and prostitution. So we sent Jennifer down there to bring her back home."

"Jennifer, are you an FBI agent also?" Emily asked totally surprised.

"Yes, I am. I had everyone fooled, didn't I?" Jennifer said with a laugh. "Don't think I didn't know what people were saying about me around town. I saw the way they crossed the street to avoid running into me."

"I feel terrible about thinking that you were just a busybody when you were really trying to help us," Liz said shaking her head.

"That's okay. That was my intent all along. No one suspected anything, and I could go around town as I pleased getting information along the way."

"So, Julia, are you ready to see Lee?" Jack asked.

"I'm ready to see that S.O.B.," Julia said getting up out of her chair.

"Let's go see what Lee has to say about this new development." Jack led the way back to the lock-up. It was like a parade with them walking single file behind him. "Wait here while I tell him he has a visitor. I can't wait to see the look on his face when he sees who it is."

Jack opened the door, and Lee began shouting at him "You have a visitor, Lee," Jack said trying to get him to quiet down.

"It had better be my lawyer, or you'll have a lawsuit on your hands," Lee yelled.

Jack opened the door and led Julia into the room. Lee's face turned pale as he saw who it was. Julia stood directly in front of him.

"What...what are you doing here?" Lee backed up into the cot and sat down.

"You bastard. You sent me to Mexico and hoped I would die down there. You didn't know that I lived for the day when I would come back here and make you pay for what you did to me." Julia was just inches from the bars of Lee's cell. She stood there with her hands clenched ready to hit him.

Jack stood next to Julia, smiling at the fact that they finally had the evidence they needed to put Lee away for good.

"You want to make that call now, Lee?"

CPSIA information can be obtained at www.ICGtesting.com
Printed in the USA
LVOW082017080812

293576LV00001B/27/P